Wild

AUTOGRAPH PAGE

To be used exclusively to recognize that special King or
Queen for their support.

This is a work of fiction. Any references or similarities to actual events, locales, real people, living or dead are intended to give the novel a sense of reality. Any similarity in other names, characters, places and incidents is entirely coincidental.

Envisions Publishing, LLC
P.O. Box 83008
Conyers, GA 30013

WILD CHERRY copyright © 2009 Jihad

ISBN: 978-0-9706102-3-2

First Printing January 2009
Printed in the United States of America

10 9 8 7 6 5 4 3 2 1

Submit Wholesale Orders to:
Envisions Publishing, LLC
P.O. Box 83008
Attn: Shipping Department
Conyers, GA 30013

Envisions
PUBLISHING COMPANY

APPRECIATION PAGE

There are so many wonderful Kings and Queens that helped make WILD CHERRY a reality, and I may miss a few but please family, chalk it up to my tired and exhausted mind.

First and foremost I wanna thank the Creator, without your inspiration and your spirit I would've given up long ago.

Thanks you Pamela Hunter over at Wake Up Publicity, wakeuppub@hotmail.com. Girl, you off the chain. Thanks for being so much more than a publicist. Thanks Reshonda for all your help and your friendship. Maurice your advice and support has been invaulable, Bridget, Jamese and everyone else that helped make Wild Cherry a reality, thank you. And a special Thanks to my niece Ronni Williams for all your help with Preacherman Blues. My sisters La-Shl, Frazier, Karen Wharton, other nieces, Lameeka Simmons, Gu-Queitz, Little, Baby, Sadaka, Shommy, thanks and push Wild Cherry like you have done my other books. I love you all.

Special thanks to the queens of J.O.W. book club in the ATL. T.C. and R.A.W. Sistahs you've supported my books since day 1, thank you, thank you so much Nova Wade, Gloria Withers and the other queens of Changing Chapterz book club in Philly. Thanks to all the queens of Turning Pages Book club in

Oakland. Thanks Lenda and the Queens of Mo' Better View Book club. Thanks Dr. Wright and the queens of Sister in the Spirit 2 book club. Thanks Tiffany and all the Memphis queens of Distinct ladies and gents.Thanks Renee and all the queens in the ATL of Circle of Sisters book club. And a very special thanks goes out to Wanda Fields, who really pushed Preacherman Blues, Thank you queen and to all the queens of Second Saturday bookclub in Atlanta. Thank you Kanika of K.O.M. book club. Thanks Ellen of Newport News and the Queens of Reading is what we do bookclub. I know I've missed several bookclubs, but I wanna thank all of you and please keep doing what you do.

And I give a very special thanks to the Kings and Queens living behind America's prison walls. Especially to all the Kings, who have supported my work and my message over the last 8 years.

By supporting my books, you help our young Brothers and sisters realize the kings and queens that they are.

Please go to <u>www.jihadwrites.com</u> to purchase an autographed copy of any of Jihad's books at a 30% discount. Allow 3-5 days for shipping. You can also send 11.99 to ENVISIONS PUBLISHING: PO box 83008, Conyers GA. And write which book you would like and the name you'd like it personalized to.

Or purchase any and all of Jihad's books in stores or online at <u>www.amazon.com</u> and please leave a review on Amazon, it may be the only way others will support Wild cherry or any of Jihad's other books. Also log on to <u>www.jihadwrites.com</u> and sign Jihad's guestbook.

Love and Life

Jihad

For more on Jihad go to www.jihadwrites.com

Also By Jihad

STREET LIFE
BABY GIRL
RIDING RHYTHM
PREACHERMAN BLUES
MVP
WILD CHERRY

Anthology:

GIGOLOS GET LONELY TOO

WILD CHERRY

<u>Prologue</u>

*T*his fool was about to make her break her promise. Cherry had told herself, no matter what, she wouldn't let anyone push her over the edge. But that was before she ran into psycho pimp.

"Tricks are for kids and I ain't the damn rabbit," Cherry calmly said. "Now unless you want me to go coo-coo all over your fat Cocoa Puff ass, you betta not call me outta my name again."

Crazy Craig pointed a finger in Cherry's direction. He was sitting at the head of the antique wood table looking like Shamu. "See, it's-it's black bitches like you," he stammered as he fingered the large diamond studded cross that dangled from his huge neck, "that cause good pimpin' to turn ugly."

Cherry forced back the thoughts that were creeping up on her. Thoughts of her teenage years when she watched her father die at the hands of four men who then went on to

1

rape and drug her. She'd done pretty good at burying their images, but the fat, sadistic pimp that was sitting in front of her, was digging those images back up.

"See what I'm sayin'?" Craig continued, crossing his arms over his huge belly. "Now, I'm trynna tell you some good shit and yo' ignant ass all zombie-eyed and shit."

He gave her a second to respond and when she didn't, he continued, "Okay, I guess you one of them new school ho's. A bitch with a brain. Well, bitch, I'm an old school pimp. A pimp with a heavy hand that will beat your brains in. You understand me, bitch?"

Cherry understood every word. And each syllable that left his mouth was pissing her off even more. One of the lessons her father had taught her before he died was that you should never let your enemies see you sweat and never let them know just how angry you are. It's a lesson her grandfather, the legendary Daddy Cool, had tried to make sure she knew as well. But the more the shirtless, freckle-faced, butter colored man spoke, the harder that rule was to follow.

Cherry glanced down at the red diamond-like glitter polish on her nails. "Ain't gon' be too many more bitches," she said, never taking her eyes off her nails.

"Bitch! Bitch! Bitch! Bitch! Black ass bitch!" he shouted.

As if they had cue cards, the three beautiful young girls at the table and the one behind Craig laughed at their boss's attempt at humor.

Cherry slowly raised her eyes back up until they met Craig's. She crossed her smooth, shiny, dark legs before pointing at him, "Maybe you didn't hear me. I'm not gon' be too many more bitches." Her words were slow and deliberate. She wanted to make sure he understood that he was about to cross into territory he might not want to cross. "See, you don't want to see the bitch in me."

"I see her," he said, his piercing eyes threatening her to continue challenging him. "And I ain't asked you to be too many more bitches." He braced both hands on the table and leaned forward, "Just be that last bitch. Bitch." He laughed.

Cherry briefly thought about her home – or the place she'd had to call home until she left two weeks ago from the Georgia Regional hospital for the criminally insane. She hated that place with a passion and didn't want to go back. That's why she'd been trying to keep a low profile, especially considering the fact that she'd escaped. But she was about to throw all caution in the wind. Oh yeah, she was about to show Craig what crazy really was.

The aroma of weed permeated the air as the girl to the right of Cherry, clad only in peach-colored panties passed her the blunt.

"Bitch, hit it," Craig said. "You might as well be high when I bust your head open."

Cherry smiled sadistically as she took the weed filled cigar from the girl, then took a long drag. She let the smoke sit in her mouth a moment, then blew it out, while she looked past the shirtless pimp, and at the life-sized black and white velvet picture that took up most of the wall behind him. Al Pacino wore a tux while holding a machine gun. The words under the picture read, *The World Is Mine*, and that's exactly the way Cherry felt as she took another pull on the Purple Haze.

"Damn, bitch, you gon' pass the dro or what?" Craig said while Dina nervously massaged his shoulders.

Cherry passed the blunt back to the girl with the peach panties, uncrossed her legs, leaned forward, and said, "I done already told you one time too many about that word."

"Get your hands off me, bitch," Craig said to Dina.

"Yes, sir, Mr. Craig," Dina said as she scurried away.

Cherry had actually met Dina a couple of days ago and after she'd shared her story, Cherry couldn't for the life of her understand why the girl hadn't stabbed Craig in his sleep.

Dina had told Cherry about one night, a month ago, when she'd returned to Craig's Victorian style home after an exhausting night of turning six tricks at a bachelor party. Craig had summoned her and she answered by saying, "What, Craig?"

Without warning he got up and with one punch to the head, knocked her out. When she awoke, she was on the living room floor, her legs spread eagle and tied to cement cinder blocks with grey duct tape. A shower rod secured to two cinderblocks prevented Dina from closing her legs. She twisted turned and screamed. "What did I do, Daddy?" she pleaded as she heard Craig's labored breathing as he approached. She almost passed out when he came into view, holding a coat hanger with a bright red tip.

"I am *Mr.* Craig, and don't you ever say *what* to me," he had said as he proceeded to brand *Mr. C* on her vagina.

And Dina wasn't the only one. From what Dina had told Cherry, they'd all been victims of Craig's wrath at one time or another. That's why Cherry couldn't understand why they stayed.

All of the women, except for Cherry jumped as Craig bounced his large frame out of the high back, throne-like red velvet chair. "Bitch! Bitch! Bitch!" He shook his head, snapping her out of her thoughts. "Bitch! Bitch! Bitch! Bitch!" He shouted like a madman.

Cherry had been in the five bedroom, broken down house with this nut and the four mentally and physically abused young women for two days and she'd had all she could take.

"Is that the mouth you used to suck your daddy's dick?" she calmly asked.

"Mr. Uhm, Mr. Craig," Dina pleaded, standing in a corner near the hole in the wall by the living room entrance, "Please, she didn't mean it. Cherry's on some type of medication."

"Dina! You went through my shit?" Cherry asked with a look of disbelief on her face as she turned toward the young girl cowering in a corner with the others.

"No, girl." Dina shook her head. "I would never do nothing like that."

"How the—"

"It wasn't me, I swear," Dina cried.

"Don't worry about her, you need to be worrying about me," Crazy Craig spat. He stood at the head of the table, cracking his knuckles. "I'm from the Ike Turner school of Beat a Bitch."

She looked at him wondering how anyone could be brainwashed by this fat, butter-yellow, hairy, lame-line tossing buddah. "I don't see how?" Cherry said.

"How what?" he asked.

"How you're from any school other than the University of baby dicks and big mouths. Shit," she reached out, picked up the blunt from where peach panties girl had set it in an ashtray, then took another pull before putting it out on the table. "Negro, my pussy lips," she coughed, "are bigger than that thing dangling from them elephant thighs of yours."

Craig looked at the girls who were snickering in the corner. "Who the fuck y'all laughin' at?"

"Nigga, you know who they laughin' at," Cherry said.

He pointed a finger at the women. "You bitches breathe a word to anyone about what y'all 'bout to see, you'll meet the same fate," he turned back to Cherry, "as this black ass bitch."

Cherry kicked off her heels before sliding the chair back from the table. She turned the chair so that it was facing the three-hundred plus pound naked madman.

"Damn, your fat ass know how to turn a woman on," she said in labored breaths while sliding her red mini up, exposing a thin mustache around her pinkish brown womanhood. "Tell Momma what your fat mini-dick ass gon' do."

The room was silent. Shock registered on the five faces that stared as Cherry began using one hand to massage her clit.

Craig turned back toward Dina. "You bring this nutty-butty bitch into my home? Whore, you just done earned yo' self a boss ass-whippin' after I finish with this bitch."

While Craig's attention was focused on Dina, Cherry slipped something from under her skirt.

"Ooh, ooh shit, you gon' fuck me up, weasel dick?" Cherry asked, getting Craig to turn his attentions back toward her.

"Nah, bitch." He shook his head. "I'm gon' send you to hell," he said cracking his knuckles again. "And after you stop breathin', I'm gon' bust a boss nut in your cold, dead pussy." Craig covered the distance that separated the two in the blink of an eye. With catlike agility, Cherry dove between his legs.

While spinning around, he shouted, "Bitch, I'm gon'...."

At the same time, the girls screamed. Craig looked down to where their eyes were focused. "You... You..." He began hyperventilating. "You...bitch."

Wild Cherry

Blood dripped from the surgeon's scalpel that Cherry held in her left hand. She stood in front of Craig, wearing a see-what-happens-when-you-fuck-with-me look on her face.

Craig fell to the floor and began crawling. Right as he grabbed her ankle, Cherry kicked his hand away.

"You cut off my..."

"Dick," she finished the sentence while the girls stared on in shock.

<u>Chapter 1</u>

" **I**ndefinitely! What does that mean?" Coach Baker shrugged his shoulders. "Son, how many times have we been down this road? How many times have I tried to get you some help?"

Jordan's eyes welled up with tears. He looked up and turned his head toward the NFC championship banners and Super Bowl trophies that adorned Coach Baker's huge colorful office. "Football is my life, Coach. I eat, drink and breathe blue and white."

Coach Baker eased his wide frame out of the peanut butter brown leather chair and walked around his cluttered office desk. "Son, your football days are over. You've been suspended three times and each time, you've denied using. The only reason you weren't out on your ass after we lost the NFC Championship game last year was because we probably wouldn't have been there if it weren't for you in the first place."

Jordan shook his head and let out a deep sigh of resignation while wondering how he could have let a little white rock ruin his career. He debated begging some more, but he knew Coach Baker, this decision was final, especially because he had been given so many chances. "I'll just go and clean out my locker."

"Already done. We've shipped everything to your home in Atlanta." The coach put a hand on Jordan's shoulder. In a calmer voice, he continued. "Son, you've been a Cowboy for four years, and three of those were Pro Bowl years. The way you ran back punts and chased down wide receivers was an art. You're the most talented athlete that I've ever coached."

"If I'm that good, then why—"

"Jordan, you're sick. Son, you need serious help with them drugs you putting in your body. They already cost you your career, next it'll be your life."

"What about the CFL? You can put in a word for me there, right Coach?"

"Son, you ain't heard a cotton-pickin' thing I done said."

"Coach, I heard you, but we talkin' about my life." He patted his chest. "My life, Coach. What am I gon' do? All I know is football."

"Dammit, Jordan." Coach Baker slammed his fleshy meathook fist onto the desk. "How long you think you'll play in Canada or overseas before the drugs cause you to embarrass yourself even more than you already have?"

"But—"

"But my white ass. Jordan, there is no way," he shook his head, "no way in Sam damn hell," the coach took a hanky from his back pocket and wiped the tears from his eyes, "I'm gon' use my influence to get you into another league so you can further embarrass me and yourself. You have not once," he grabbed Jordan shoulders, "not one

damn time acknowledged that you even have a problem."
He paused to get his emotions under control. "That's step
one. After you acknowledge that you have a problem, then
you have to want to get better, and even then you have to
get on your knees and beg the Man upstairs to deliver you
from your drug-induced hell."

Chapter 2

"*C*an you believe that old-ass hillbilly had the audacity to tell me," he stopped pacing and patted his muscular bare chest, "Jordan 'Bullet' mothafuckin' Hayes, the baddest man to ever step foot on a football field, to get on my knees and pray? Hmmmph. Jordan Hayes don't bow down or kneel to nothin', especially God. Hell, He the reason..." Jordan lit the burnt glass pipe and took a long pull. A few seconds passed before he allowed the white smoke to escape from his lungs. He looked around the small hotel room. "Now, what the hell was I sayin'?"

"Same shit you been sayin' since I started fuckin' wit' yo' forever-high ass a couple months ago," Cherry said rising from between China Doll's long, tanned legs.

Ignoring her outburst, Jordan continued. "Oh yeah, I know what the hell I was sayin'." He paused trying to think of what he had just remembered. "Got damn, bigmouth, big lipped bitch, you done made me forget what I just remembered."

11

"If you see a bitch," Cherry was now sitting at the edge of the queen sized hotel bed with her arms crossed, "I suggest you slap a bitch, nigga. Besides, that shit happened a damn year ago. How many times I have to listen to that same old bullshit?"

Jordan looked over at the three beautiful women on the queen-size bed at the Downtown Motel 6. "I'm 'bout tired of that mouth, Sweetness."

Cherry licked her large puffy lips. "Well, put somethin' in it, you pretty-dick bastard."

He started running his hand up and down the shaft of his already long, growing, hook-shaped manhood, while Cherry sat on the bed smiling.

As if they were the only two in the room, China Doll and Little Woman continued kissing, licking, and massaging each other while Jordan took three long strides over to the bed.

"Sweetness, get ready to choke."

"Get to chokin'," Cherry said as she hungrily took his pulsating, almond-colored dick into her mouth.

"Ahh shit. Suck it, bitch. Suck the skin off this mothafucka'," Jordan commanded.

"Daddy, you want me to get your shit?" Little Woman, the twenty-year-old Drew Barrymore, babyfaced white girl, looked up and asked.

"Yeah, Sweetness, and get a big one," he said before turning his attention to the tall Kimora Lee-looking China Doll. "Get the cough drops and get your ass over here, girl."

A minute later, China Doll was licking his ass lollipop-style and playing with his balls like a set of dice as he put the glass dick to his lips and inhaled. The little white rock disintegrated before his eyes. As he swallowed smoke,

Cherry swallowed the thick creamy liquid that exploded from his manhood.

"Mothafuck, son of a, shit, fire, damn!" He shouted. "Y'all musta..." he panted trying to catch his breath, "took a life insurance policy out on my ass," he said as he pushed Cherry from between his legs.

"You gon' wish I did if you don't serve this pussy," Cherry said. "I wanna feel all five miles of that hook dick in me," she said, massaging the reddened head of his dick.

"Little Woman, bring me a glove," Jordan said.

Cherry gripped both her hands around Jordan's tight, round, muscular ass. Before Little Woman could respond, she arched her back and pulled Jordan inside.

"You nasty whore. You nasty, stank-ass whore," China Doll erupted. "I don't want your pussy juice inside me."

Cherry opened her mouth to respond, but only grunts came out. Jordan's ass cheeks flexed; sweat ran down his chest and between the ripples of his stomach muscles as he slowly took all of his dick out and slammed it back and forth inside Cherry's ravenous, wet womanhood.

"That's some fucked up shit, whore," China Doll continued as she stood in front of the bed with her hands on her hips. "How you gon' hog the dick and take it raw, knowing I want a piece of his ass?"

Jordan was about to pile-drive his dick inside Cherry once again when, in one thrust, she pushed him to the side.

"What the?" Jordan shouted, as he rolled off the bed.

"On everything I love," Cherry pointed a bright red nail at China Doll, "I swear ta God, you keep running that dick sucker of yours, I'll put my fist—"

"Bitch, who—"

"Nah," Cherry interrupted before China Doll could finish, "who the fuck *you* think *you* dealin' with?

Furthermore, I don't play that bitch shit, so you need to watch what comes outta that nasty ass mouth of yours." Turning her attention to Jordan, who was getting the last rock from the nightstand, she said, "That right there," she pointed, "is my dick, whore. Now, I chose to share his ass with you two tricks 'cause that's what *he* wanted. Now, you can lick his ass, massage his shoulders, whatever the fuck, but I'm the only flag going up and down that pole," Cherry said.

He dropped his pipe and the small diamond-shaped rock. "Son of a fuck." Jordan fell to his knees. His eyes were only inches from the floor when he started crawling around the dark room. "Y'all done made me drop my shit."

Cherry looked up just in time to see Little Woman placing something inside her purse.

"Oh hell nah," Cherry jumped up from the bed, "It ain't even goin' down like that, bitch," Cherry said, kicking the petite little white girl in the head. "Bitch, you done lost your damn mind, stealin' from my man." She grabbed a lock of the girl's dirty blonde hair. "Don't worry, bitch, I'm gon' help you find it."

"No, I-I, stop," the small white girl shouted as Cherry hit the girl in the mouth with a closed fist.

Oblivious to the melee, Jordan was still crawling on the floor frantically searching for his drugs.

China Doll grabbed Cherry.

"Jordan, the bitch got my hair," Cherry shouted as China doll dragged Cherry off of Little Woman.

His eyes lit up like he'd found the Hope Diamond when he spotted what looked like his drugs.

"Get my blade. Get my got-damn blade," China Doll shouted at Little Woman, who was at the TV stand going through her friend's knock-off Louis Vuitton handbag.

14

Jordan was flat on his stomach, despite the darkness that blanketed the room he somehow spotted the dime-size half an eight ball crack rock under the bed.

"Jordan!" Cherry screeched.

He grabbed the rock, slid from under the bed and sat at the edge with his pipe.

"Jordan, the bitch got a knife," Cherry moaned.

He looked up, even tried to get up, but the pipe told him differently.

"Do it! Do it!" China Doll ordered Little Woman, who was holding the red Swiss army knife in the air.

"Noooooooo!" Cherry shouted as Little Woman sliced her face from the left eye down to the right side of her upper lip.

Chapter 3

"**W**ho's your daddy?" Jevon asked as he rammed his massive shaft into the woman. She might have been no more than five-feet-two and about thirty pounds heavier than he liked them, but this chick knew how to ride Mr. Magic.

"Oh, my pussy just loves that big, black dick," Sharon said, her reddish brown shoulder length hair going every which way as she bounced up and down on Jevon's long polish sausage-shaped member.

His hands grasped her love handles. "I said, who's your damn daddy?" Jevon's neck and biceps flexed as he lifted Sharon up and down onto him with precision and finesse.

"You are, Daddy," Sunny said as she climbed onto the queen-size ten year old worn out mattress supported by gray cinder blocks and two box springs.

"Woman, I wasn't talkin' to your freaky ass," Jevon admonished.

"Oh. Okay." She smiled. "Sorry."

Determined not to let Sunny's ignorance ruin the moment, he said, "You see your sister ridin' Mr. Magic."

Sharon was too busy slopping pussy juice everywhere to pay attention to Jevon and her sister.

"Damn, woman, slow your ass down. Fuck you tryin' ta do, kill my dick?" Jevon said to Sharon while watching her hair go everywhere and her 38 DD's fly up and down.

"No! No! Oh! Oh! Wait! Wait!" Sharon panted as her sister climbed over Jevon's head and mounted his face.

A minute later, both sisters where in the throes of passion. "Ooh, ahh, that's it, lick my clit, baby. Oh yeah, Daddy. I love the way you... Oh yeah, that's it. Stick your finger, stick it in my ass daddy," Sunny crooned.

Jevon never had a problem getting it up, but for these two freaky-ass sisters, he had to pop a Viagra to keep it up.

"Oh, Oh, Daddy, I'm, I'm..." Sunny spasmed and squeezed her thighs tight around Jevon's head.

He bucked and jerked, trying to break free. Trying to breathe.

"AHHHHHHHHHHHHH!!!!" Sunny screamed as she exploded, a stream of cum shooting into his mouth and all over his face.

Sunny rolled off of him and onto the floor. "You crazy-ass freak! Fuck's your—" he coughed, "problem?" He bucked, throwing Sharon off of him.

"Shit!" she screamed trying to break her fall as she, too, rolled onto the apartment's nasty, worn gray carpeted floor.

Both sisters looked up dumbfounded.

Jevon sat up on the mattress, coughing and wiping his shiny face with the checkerboard bed sheet. "First you try to break my dick." He looked over at Sharon. "And you," he sat at the edge of the mattress pointing at Sunny, "bitch, you tried to smother..." he coughed again, "and then drown me. You know you a squirter. Sunny, why would you cum on my face?"

"I-I don't know." She shrugged her pale shoulders. "I couldn't help it."

"I feel like you peed on my face. Fuck," he shouted.

"God," Sharon looked over at her younger sister. "You always find a way to ruin a fuck. I was on nut number seven," Sharon said to her younger sister with an exasperated look on her face.

"I'm sorry. You guys know how I get. I-I can't help it. Nobody has ever made my kitty cat meow like you do, Daddy," Sunny said.

"Fuck it. You two go get cleaned up; we need to go over the plan again."

While the two sisters were in the shower, Jevon went through their purses, stealing a few dollars here and there. Afterward, the thought of showering crossed his mind, but then he looked around the small two bedroom apartment and thought that there was no way he was going to take a shower in an apartment that was nastier than a gas station bathroom.

These two sisters were by far the freakiest women he'd ever fucked. He shook his head as he remembered meeting Sharon six months ago at the bank were she had just been promoted to head teller. Sharon, a big Dallas Cowboy fan, immediately recognized him, thinking he was his twin brother, Jordan. And as usual he let her think just that. Sharon was not his type. She was short and dumpy-looking, but she was new pussy, and that was more important than being his type.

*****

18

About five, six months ago, Jevon did what he and Jordan called pussy pre-qualification for two nights - feeling her out, asking sexual questions to gauge whether or not he could hit it on the first date. Obviously, she passed the test, because he not only ended up taking a white woman out, but a short, dumpy white woman at that. He took her to a Red Lobster way out in redneck country, because if Jordan or any of his other boys got wind of the polar bugga bear he was with, he'd never live it down. Sharon couldn't even have made the cut for a two-in-the-morning-half-drunk-at-the club-last-piece-of-pussy-in-the-house-lay. The only reason he picked her up was because she was white, and he was bored.

That entire evening, and for the next couple days he kept up the farce of being his brother. At the end of the first night, he'd taken her back to the apartment she shared with her sister, Sunny.

"Can I use your restroom?" he'd asked while they stood at her apartment door.

"Sure," she'd said.

The old can-I-use-your-restroom trick was the quickest and easiest way to get into a girl's place, he thought as he made his way to where she'd pointed. A couple minutes later, while rummaging through the bathroom cabinets, he had heard the faint sound of someone moaning. Lucky for him, he didn't have to use the restroom, so the toilet flushing wouldn't alert the person moaning in the next room. He crept out of the restroom and took a couple steps to the door attached to the room from which the moaning came. He slowly turned the knob and gently opened it.

"Oh Lord. I done died and went to white ho' heaven," he'd said to himself. He could barely believe his eyes. A tall Wonder Woman fine white broad had her muscular legs spread eagle on the bedroom wall, back on the bed, her long red hair draped over the full-size mattress, falling just short of the floor. A big black dildo made a buzzing sound as it vibrated inside her mouth, while both her hands were making piston-like movements between her legs. Her stiff pink nipples had to be an inch long.

He stripped naked right there in the hall, walked into the room and...

Jevon was just about to cum again just from the six month old memory, but Sharon walked into the room. She wore only a white towel, tied around her ample waist, which she let fall to the floor as she climbed back onto the bed. "Jordan, you're still naked." Sharon ran a fingernail slightly down the shaft of his member. "Ahh, did Mr. Magic miss mommy?" she asked, bending her head down toward Jevon's erect member.

"Yeah, but we have business to discuss," he said, jumping up and running into the bathroom where Sunny was applying makeup.

He looked at her perfect tanned white ass, wondering what the fuck had happened to her homely, flat-assed, funny-shaped sister.

Fifteen minutes later, the three of them sat at the apartment's glass-topped kitchen table.

Jevon still couldn't believe his luck. He'd hit the poo-nanny jackpot and was about to break the bank. It had taken him six weeks to convince Sharon and her sister to go along with his plan, and another four months of dotting the i's and crossing all the t's.

"It just doesn't seem right." Sharon shook her head. "Jevon Hayes, have you even heard a word I've said?" she asked.

"The dead, two states over heard you woman," he said, catching the tail end of Sharon's soliloquy.

"I mean, he's your twin," Sharon said as she crossed her legs, a Newport dangling from her lips.

"Yeah. And you two are brothers," Sunny interjected.

Jevon and Sharon just stared at her with a shut-the-fuck-up look on their faces.

"What did I say? You *are* brothers," Sunny said.

Ignoring her, Jevon said, "It don't seem right for you two to fuck me sideways at the same time in the same bed. But you have been for damn near six months now." He smiled. "So, Sharon, don't talk to me about right and wrong."

"I'm not setting my sister up to go to prison," Sharon replied.

"I'm not setting Jordan up either. He's just the fall guy in case the cops come after me." He pointed a finger in the air. "*In case.*"

"Okay, then, a fall guy. It just doesn't seem right and it definitely doesn't feel right."

He looked over at Sunny. She wore a silly grin on her face as she shrugged indifference.

Turning back to Sharon, he continued, "Let me worry about what feels right. For the last damn time, my brother is nothing and has nothing. You understand me? He lives with me, and he drives around all day, every day, knocking on doors begging people to let him do their yard work. My brother, NFL great, Jordan 'Bullet' Hayes, raking yards and cutting grass. He was all that and a thousand bags of chips when he played for the Cowboys, but that was two years ago. He's a geek monster, a crackhead, a base master. He's nothing."

Sharon interrupted. "And what does his drug problem have to do with what we're planning to do to him?"

Jevon put his hands over his face and shook his head. "First, *we* are not planning to do anything to him. And second, what is with you all of a sudden? We've only been planning and working out the kinks for four months now."

Sharon shook her head. "I just don't see why..."

"I already explained why."

"Well, please explain it to me one more time?" Sharon tapped the pencil on the tablet in front of her while looking at him sideways.

Speaking slowly Jevon began. "My brother, has nothing, okay? He's never been locked up, so under the federal sentencing guidelines, the most he'll do for unarmed bank robbery, *if* he's apprehended and convicted is five years. I'm hitting the shipment next month on the thirteenth, two days before yearly bonuses go out to the GM plant employees; and since your branch services them, you said yourself, they'll order anywhere from a quarter mil to a half million dollars. A quarter mil of that will put me all the way in the game. And, again," he pointed a finger in the air, "*If* Jordan goes down, by the time he gets out I'll be rich."

"You can't be sure of that," Sharon said.

"Hell, if I can't. You heard of Bishop TJ Money, right?"

"Who hasn't?" Sharon said.

Sunny pointed. "I know Bishop Money. He did the rap video with Dollar Bill and Fifty."

"I don't know about that, but I do know that Bishop Money pulled some strings and got Bishop CW's land rezoned. And CW just got the go ahead to begin building the Conyers Center City Mall. And check this out. They ain't even broke ground yet and we already got commitments for over thirty percent of the retail space. And if something did go wrong CW is guaranteeing my money with the Sunday offerings. You know how big Beautiful Baptist is. Now, tell me my money ain't guaranteed."

"Tell me you did not tell Bishop Wiley what we're planning?" Sharon said.

"Come on now, the man's a bishop."

"And that means?"

"Why you all up in mine?" Jevon stood up from the table, angry at himself for talking too much. "You just do your part." He patted his chest. "I got this," he said with way more passion then he felt. "Now can we go over the plan again, please?" he asked, scooting the kitchen chair closer to Sharon.

"The Wells Fargo armored truck will pull up between ten and eleven AM. The truck will be parked here." Sharon drew a diagram of the truck and the rear of the bank. "The guard in the passenger's seat will get out. The driver will watch through his sideview mirror as the other guard walks to the back and opens the truck's rear door. Then, the guard riding in the back with the money will get out with three or four bags. The driver will cover them as they make their way into the bank's rear entrance."

Jevon threw his hands in the air. "Got damn, woman. I'm putting my life on the line and you're skipping over details. Fuck," he shouted.

"Don't curse at me Jevon Hayes. Don't friggin' curse at me. I'm sorry. We've only gone over this a million times, the last couple months. You should know your part."

"I do, but we need to go over it a million more times until we cover every single damn detail."

"Okay, already. I'll back up," she said, looking at Sunny for support and getting nothing but a blank stare. "Four minutes after the Wells Fargo truck pulls into the bank parking lot, you leave the Chevron gas station across the street and pull up in the stolen car. You park in a handicapped space and limp through the bank's front door. By then Tonetta, the bank's Branch manager and I will have signed off on the delivery and the guards will be leaving. I'll engage Tonetta in conversation, distracting her and buying thirty seconds before she hits the vault timer. That's when you step over to the vault and pull the jacket with the water gun. You explain to Tonetta that you have kidnapped Tangia and Treyon from Urban Prep Early Childhood Academy, and if she doesn't open the vault gate they will be dead before the first police siren can be heard in the distance."

Jevon interrupted. "And then, I grab the bags, tell her if I don't get a five minute start, her kids will be dead before the cops catch me."

"That's the part I'm uncomfortable with," Sharon said.

"Sharon, you know good and got damn well, I'm not going anywhere near her damn kids. What the fuck is there to feel uncomfortable about?"

"It's just the point of using her kids as leverage. I feel bad enough about giving you the info on them as it is."

"Get over it. Your branch manager will find out soon enough that her children are fine. By then, I will have spit on the water gun, and have thrown it in the bushes outside the bank."

"That's another thing."

"What?" Jevon asked in an exasperated tone.

"The spit."

"I already explained." He smiled. "Identical twins share the same DNA. If, and I emphasize the *if,* shit gets hot, I will lead the cops to Jordan and they will have a perfect DNA match."

Jevon felt like his plan was near fool-proof. The problem was the two women sitting in front of him. If he didn't have everything down to a tee, they'd be the ones to mess everything up.

Chapter 4

"*T*here is only one," Dr. Cheyenne Jamison held a manicured finger in the air, "guarantee in this life. Unfortunately for everyone in this room, death will be expedited by drug use." She slowly walked around the circle of chairs and faces that spanned three generations; black and white men and women from 17 to 72 sat in the circle holding on to her every word. "The next time the bottle, the pipe, or whatever you're addicted to starts calling, don't answer. That is," she paused for emphasis, "if you have one thing, just one thing, to live for." She stood in the middle of the circle, scanning the forty eyes that stared back. Finally, her eyes rested on a hazel-eyed newcomer to the Y's Thursday night NA meeting.

"Mr. Hayes, would you care to share?" Dr. Jamison asked.

Why am I nervous? Jordan asked himself. This was the fourth Narcotics Anonymous chapter he had joined over the past seven months. He'd lost his home, his money everything. Even the little money he was supposed to receive from the NFL went to paying off an astronomical debt to the IRS. Drugs had destroyed his life and the lives of everyone around him. He still had nightmares of that night in that Motel 6, almost a year ago. And he still prayed that Cherry had survived the attack.

"Mr. Hayes? Are you okay?" the part-time group psychiatrist asked.

Jordan took in the doctor's appearance. She was okay, definitely not a dime, but she was a strong nickel, and a couple pennies. She was the epitome of class. She strolled around the room with the grace of a queen. With his head down, Jordan slowly rose from the metal fold-up chair and took a couple steps toward the middle of the circle. The words "I'm sorry" escaped his lips, as if a silent call for mercy and forgiveness.

"Take your time, baby," a middle-aged, graying, heavyset motherly-looking, black woman said.

"My name is... My name is Jordan Hayes, and..." He paused. "And I'm a crack addict."

"I knew it." A brotha stood up and pointed. "Jordan 'The Bullet' Hayes. Man, you were a wide receiver's nightmare. In 1997, your rookie year, you scored eight touchdowns on defense, shattering the NFL record."

A brief smile creased Jordan's lips. "Yeah, that was seven years ago, but now," he held his head up, "this is me." His voice went up several octaves. "A twenty-seven-year-old crack addict. I've been clean for over nine months."

The forty addicts surrounding him applauded.

"But I still feel dirty." He turned to Dr. Jamison, thinking that she even crossed her legs with class. "My friend, lover, comforter, my God was crack-cocaine." He turned back toward the others sitting in the chairs circling the large room inside the Butler Street YMCA.

"I started getting high my second year in the league, and I stayed high up until," he looked at the beads of blue balls stitched into the old dirty carpeted floor, "nine months ago. I was naked in a motel with three women. I sat in a corner watching a woman get beat and carved up by two prostitutes. I didn't move, just listened to my pipe and kept smoking. To this very day I don't know what happened to that woman. I tried to find her, but all I had was her first name, and I don't even know if Cherry was her real name."

Jordan was in tears as he continued. "She might even be dead. I could've stopped them. I could've saved her."

*****

Jordan stood across the room away from where all the attendees were enjoying refreshments and standing around talking after the NA meeting. Every time he spoke at groups like NA, Jordan let his emotions takeover and at the end he always felt like a heavy weight had been lifted from his soul. Things were so much clearer now that he was clean. He was confident that he could take on anything and come out on top.

Before he heard her birdlike voice, he felt her hands on the back of his arms. "Well, hell-the-fuck-o Mr. Football man," she whispered into his ear. "My pussy got so wet listening to the passion with which you spoke."

He turned to face the voice that caused his manhood to stir.

"You like?" She smiled as she watched his eyes go from her red heels up her long shapely legs, to her black-girl hips, small waist, olive-white face, and shoulder-length red hair. "I bet that big black dick you got hiding in those jeans would love to come out and play with Ms. Kitty."

"Sunny, please, this is an NA meeting, not a pick up joint."

Dr. Jamison seemed to appear from nowhere. For some odd reason Jordan felt embarrassed. Embarrassed in a way that a black man feels when bringing a white woman, for the first time, to a social function with a room full of sistas.

She pouted. "Ms. Jamison, stop being such a party pooper. I was just..."

"*Dr*. Jamison," she corrected. "And, Sunny, I know what you were *just* doing."

"God, what does a sister have to do to meet a nice brother?" Sunny turned and walked off in a way that caused her already too short pink and red paisley mini skirt to rise. And Sunny didn't even try to pull it down.

"First, you have to be a sista," Dr. Jamison said before looking up at Jordan. "Tell me I didn't just say that out loud."

Jordan just stood there, looking like a six-foot-four, 225-pound smirking kid.

"Well? Say something," Dr. Jamison said.

"You are absolutely beautiful."

"Flattery will get you everywhere, but bullshit will get you a shovel."

"Say agin?"

"Bullshit, Mr. Hayes." She pointed to Sunny, who had now found another victim. "Sunny is beautiful. I'm just ordinary."

"First, Miss Lady." Jordan put a hand over his mouth. "Oops! I'm sorry. I meant Miss *Dr*. Lady," he joked. "*Mr*. Hayes was my father, and second," he pointed two fingers at her, "there's nothing ordinary about you. And for the record, I have nothing against white women. At one time I was partial to anything other than a black woman. But now that I'm clean and my vision isn't blurred, the only thing a white woman can do for me is lead me to a sista. And if I may say so myself and mind you, this is real talk," he paused as he looked deep into the doctor's eyes, "You have something that can't be taught or surgically implanted."

"And what would that be, Mr. Man?"

"C-L-A-S-S."

"And how would you know that?"

"As you have your doctorate in Psychology, I have my doctorate in Classology, graduated magna-cum-oh-laudy-thank-you-Jesus from Sidewalk University."

"Jordan Hayes, you are a fool." She laughed. "I just came over to save you from," she looked over to where Sunny was, "Jaws. And..." She placed her hand on his. Their eyes locked and a sort of warm, tingly sensation shot through Jordan's body, before she jerked her hand away and turned her head.

An uncomfortable minute of silence passed between them. Both of them looked around the room, avoiding eye contact with each other. Finally, Jordan broke the silence. "Are you okay?"

"I'm fine." She looked at the floor before asking, "Do you have a sponsor?"

"I have two." He paused. "Are you leaving now?"

Her eyes still on the floor, she said, "No, I have some paperwork to finish up."

"Oh, okay. I guess, uhm, I'll see you next Thursday," he said turning to leave.

"So, you're coming to the next meeting?" She sounded anxious.

Jordan turned, shrugging his shoulders. "Only time will tell."

Wild Cherry

His smile. The rhythm with which he moved. His cool calmness. Who was this man? And why am I even asking myself these questions. I'm a professional, a psychiatrist and he's, he's, I don't know who or what he is. I can't be doing this, she said to herself while watching him walk away.

Chapter 5

*T*he downtown Atlanta streets, particularly on Auburn and Butler where the Y was located, were alive with twenty-dollar hookers competing with ten-dollar crack whores trying to catch a trick outside of the well-lit, all-night Church's Chicken. Across the street from Church's at the American Legion, old men drifted in and out. It was bingo night for some and Viagra-trick-with-a-young-whore night for others.

Jordan stopped, took a deep breath and looked up to the heavens. The sky was a dark clear dance floor, sparkling with stars and constellations.

He'd walked a couple blocks when his instincts kicked in. He had a strange feeling that he was being followed. He took a few more steps before quickly turning around. A late model gold Nissan Sentra with blacked-out windows and oversized chrome wheels pulled up.

Before the driver's window came down, Snoop and Dre's classic hit, *Murder was the Case,* blasted from the car's sound system.

Wild Cherry

"Hey there, football man. Need a lift?" Sunny asked as the driver's window descended.

He shook his head. "Nah, sweetie, I'm good. It's a beautiful April night. I'm just gon' get my walk on."

"Now, I knows a big ole strong man like you ain't 'fraid uh no little ole country white girl like me, is you?" Sunny batted her eyelids.

He shook his head. "Girl, you just don't know. If I didn't have so much on my mind."

"You'd what? Finish. What would you do, Mr. Football man?" She licked her lips. "What would you do if you didn't have so much on your mind?"

"You just don't know."

"I will when you tell me."

"Let me put it this way. As long as it's been since I had a woman, you'd have an ussy when I finished with you."

"An ussy?"

"I'd fuck the P off the word."

"Oh shit, daddy." She licked her bright pink lips again. "My kitty is wet all over again." She put her arm out the window beckoning him over. "Come here, just for a second."

He looked around as cars passed by the downtown street.

She shook her head. "I ain't gon' bite," she paused, "well, that is, unless you want me to."

A moment later, his arms were braced on her door as he leaned over the driver's side window.

"See this?" Her skirt was rolled up on her waist and she had two fingers slowly rubbing up and down her love nest. "Jordan, I want you to meet Ms. Kitty. Meow," she purred.

Jordan just stared.

"Don't act like you ain't never seen no waxed pink kitty cat." She paused. "Oh, I get it. Cat literally got your tongue. Well, the cat can have the tongue; Ms. Kitty wants that monster you got caged behind your zipper." She looked out the window at the print in his jeans. "For a minute, back at the meeting, I didn't think you liked white meat, but I see I was wrong."

A flash of light interrupted the moment. "Move along," a voice boomed from a loud speaker behind them.

Jordan turned to see a police car behind Sunny's Nissan. When he turned back around she'd pulled off. He was relieved the police had come. If they hadn't, there was no telling what he would've done.

Jordan breathed in the downtown cool air, as he enjoyed the serenity of common noise as he referred to all the sounds heard while walking the Atlanta night downtown streets. The same streets that not to long ago he'd woke up on after many all-night drug binges.

He hadn't known her before that night and they'd only had about a ten-minute conversation, but Jordan couldn't get Dr. Jamison off of his mind. He hadn't known what he wanted in a woman until he'd met her.

Since the day Cherry was beaten and carved up, Jordan hadn't touched another woman. And in one night he'd fallen in love with a sister he didn't even know and was about to fuck the brains out of a pink-toe he'd only just met.

"Doctor, Doctor, what it be? What it be?" A black man of indeterminable age wearing several pairs of dirty pants and shirts walked up.

"It be, what it is?" Jordan replied.

"Doctor, let me squeeze your brain for just one," the dirty little man pointed a dark finger in the late night air, "minute. Just one, sixty-second minute. Can you give me that, Doctor?"

Jordan smiled before nodding. "Go ahead," he said, leaning against a light pole.

"Yeah, yeah, Doctor, okay. Here we go. Here we go. If you were to die today, I mean, right now, right here, this second, how would you be remembered? Can you answer me that?"

Jordan put his hand under his chin, and for a few seconds, he contemplated what the man had asked. He shrugged his shoulders. "You know what?"

"Yeah, Doctor. I know what and I know why but the question is," he jabbed Jordan in the chest, "do you?"

"I don't. I'm just trynna make it to tomorrow," Jordan said.

"Ain't nobody promised a tomorrow. Doctor, you better focus on making today your best day. That said, answer me one more thing. Can you do that, Doctor?"

"Shoot."

"Can a good brotha borrow one dollar? Just one single, solitary dollar," the man asked.

Jordan pulled out his wallet, thinking the man in front of him was crazy but at the same time wise beyond his years, whatever they were. "I want it back next week," he said, "or I'm charging interest," Jordan joked as he handed the man half the money he had on him.

"No problem, Doctor. I got you." He said putting the five-dollar bill Jordan had handed him to his nose. "Yes, sir, Doctor. I'm gon' get you back next week." The man turned and began walking away. "When I see you again, I need you to answer me that question, okay? Can you do me that? Can you?"

"Yeah, I got you." Jordan smiled, thinking that whenever he thought of how bad he had it, God always threw someone in his path that had it worse.

He looked up. "You real funny."

"Who are you speaking to?"

Jordan jumped, stumbling and barely catching himself before falling to the sidewalk.

"You all right?" she asked, helping him to his feet.

"Woman, I mean, Dr. Jamison, you scared ten years off my life."

She was bent over laughing, her fingers entwined around the gray metal chain link fence that surrounded the old abandoned building they stood in front of.

"I don't see anything funny," he said.

"That's because you didn't see yourself speaking to the sky one minute and the next, jumping up and coming down, falling over your own big feet."

They both laughed.

"I was driving home when I saw you talking to a street person. I didn't want to interrupt so I pulled over and parked over there," she pointed to the IHOP restaurant parking lot across the street. "That was real nice of you to give that man some money."

"It's a loan," he pointed out. "I didn't *give* anyone anything."

"Yeah, right." She smiled while giving him a sideways glance.

"Okay," he shrugged his shoulders, "so I'm a sucker for a person in need."

She held her hand out. "In that case."

He took her outstretched hand in his. "It's a beautiful night, you wanna take a walk. I'd love to show you a different side of downtown, one you probably haven't seen."

"I seriously doubt that. Contrary to the way I look and speak, I grew up in the Techwood projects. They were maybe two or three miles from where we are standing."

"I would have never guessed. But, there are places and things I'd like to show you that you can't access by car. And as you know with all the urban development going on, the city changes every year," he said.

She pointed across the street. "What about my car?"

He looked at the convertible BMW parked in the front of IHOP. "It'll be okay. IHOP doesn't close and you parked it where people on the inside can see it."

"I'm not worried about it getting vandalized or stolen. I'm worried about it getting towed or booted."

"See that red Toyota." He pointed a few spaces down from Dr. Jamison's beamer. That's mine. I leave it in the IHOP lot all the time. It's the only free parking downtown. Our little secret." He winked. "Besides, I have to walk you back anyways to get my little hoopty.

Chapter 6

Sitting on the black leather couch in his brother's basement apartment, Jordan couldn't help but think about his evening with Cheyenne. He could hardly believe they'd walked and talked half the night away. It was the best three hours he'd ever spent. Being with Dr. Cheyenne Jamison felt better than the day he was drafted into the NFL, or any game he'd scored the winning touchdown in.

The doorbell interrupted his thoughts.

As he got up from the couch, the news ticker going across the TV screen caught his eye.

The search continues for a man who robbed the North Druid Hills Bank of America branch with what police now know was a Fisher Price water gun.

On the way to answer the door, Jordan stopped to secure the towel wrapped around his waist. He looked at his watch. *2:47a.m.* "What kind of idiot would rob a bank with a watergun?"

Jordan had been home just long enough to have taken a shower and to have caught a quick minute of World News.

Probably one of Jevon's harem, Jordan thought as he reached for the doorknob.

"Sunny?"

She licked her candy-apple red lipstick lips before pushing the door open. Without a word she dropped to her knees, yanked the towel off of him and wrapped her lips around Jordan's manhood.

Move away. Shut the door. Tell her you live with your twin brother. These thoughts crossed his mind, but thoughts were all they were. Jordan was paralyzed. He couldn't do anything but enjoy the white woman on her knees, bobbing her head up and down.

"Shit, damn, fuck, oh my damn," he said, catching a sudden case of Tourette's syndrome. He wrapped a lock of her red hair around his fist.

"Uhmm,Uhmmmm,Uhmmmmmmmmmmmmmmmm," she hummed, causing a vibrating sensation as she worked mouth and tongue around his steel-hard member.

A few minutes later, Jordan's neck muscles bulged. The ripples in his stomach flexed. His legs began to vibrate.

"Uhm, Uhm, explode," she spoke between piston-like head movements, "in my mouth."

He grabbed the back of her head and squeezed, shooting nine months of built-up cum into her mouth. Without a word passing between the two, he spun around, got on his knees, and pushed her back toward the gray carpet. "Fuck," he said jumping up. "Right back," he said running to his room.

"What's wrong?" she shouted.

He rummaged through his top drawer next to his bed. "Magnum," he shouted, finding the black and gold box of condoms.

Moments later, her skirt was pulled up. She was on her knees, and Jordan's large hands were gripped around her small waist. She moaned in ecstasy as he rested on his knees behind her, lifting her frame up and down off of his diamond-hard dick.

"Oh, oh, oh, you're, you're, oh shit, oh, not so hard, fuck, you're too, too big," she panted.

"Nah, sweetness, you wanted this dick. Now take it," he said slapping her pink ass.

"Oh shit, fuck, Jor-Jor-Jordan, I'm cum-cum-cummin', I'm cumminnnnnnnnnnnn'," she shouted.

She tried to get away, but Jordan had the grip of life around her waist as he continued sliding in and out, playing her body like a good jazzman blowing his horn.

Not even a minute passed before she again went to hollerin, "Oh shit, got damn, I'm, I'm cummin, oh shit, I feel you in my stomach. Fuck me, fuck me, fuck me, yeah, yeah, oh, oh, I'm cummmmmmmmiiiiiiiinnnnn," she screamed.

While she caught her breath, Jordan stood up, pulled Sunny to her feet, lifted her so her legs were wrapped around his neck and shoulders. Her hands were kneading and massaging his bald head while he sucked and tongue loved on and around her moist womanhood. Slowly, he carried her across the room to the far wall. In no time her legs had gone from his shoulders to now being wrapped around his 34 inch waist. At first he massaged the area around her throbbing clit with his marble hard manhood.

"Huhhhhhhhhhhhhhhhh!" she gasped as Jordan slammed himself as far as he could inside of her. Tears were in her eyes. "No one... has... ever made me... cum so hard... and so many times," she panted.

"This is what you wanted? Little white girl wanna big buck nigga dick up inside you? Don't you? Huh? You can go tell Buffy, Hilary and your other lily white friends how it feels to be fucked by a big buck black man," he said between thrusting in and out of her.

"Oh my Lord," she panted. "I can't, I can't cum anymore. I, I..."

"You like this dick. You like the way I tap that ass, don't you?"

"Yes, yes," she said, tears running down her face.

"You wanna know why they call me Bullet?" he said between slow, measured powerful thrusts.

"Uh-hmm." She nodded and purred.

"You sure? You think you ready to go where no dick has ever taken you before?"

"Yes! Yes! Yes! Beam me up! Beam me up, Daddy."

Jordan smiled as he bent his knees, flexed his calf muscles and rammed himself in and out of her at an impossible speed.

"I-I-I-I-cum-cum-cum-in-in-in," she shouted over and over, cumming back to back, multiple times.

Moments later, Sunny fainted from extreme pleasure. Before Jordan had a chance to revive her, the apartment door came flying open. Jordan turned just in time to be staring down the barrel of a gun.

"On the floor! Hands behind your head! Now!" A cop shouted, while another kicked Jordan in the back.

Chapter 7

*S*treams of sweat rolled off of Jevon's forehead. For weeks he'd rehearsed what he was going to say when this very moment came up. The pressure was mounting and he felt guilty, but there was nothing he could do other than what he had done. He looked Jordan in the eye through the plate glass that separated detainee and civilian. "I fucked up. I fucked up real bad."

"No shit!" Jordan spoke through the black phone."

"I don't-I'm—"

"Jevon Hayes?" Jordan shook his head. "You are a fucking idiot," he whispered. "Idiot! Idiot! Idiot!" He punched the glass wall separating him from his sniveling brother. "After all the shit I've been through, you go and rob a fucking bank."

Tears welled up in Jevon's eyes, not for robbing the bank but for robbing Jordan of his freedom. He spoke into the visiting room phone. "I felt my world—our world—closing in on us. How do you think it makes me feel knowing you driving around in your little Toyota with a lawnmower hanging out of the hatchback." Jevon used his sleeve to wipe the tears from his face. "You... NFL great, my brother, my twin, out there beggin' folks to cut they grass. Why? Why humiliate yourself like that? Haven't you been through enough?"

"Obviously not. I'm in here."

"I know. I know." Jevon shook his head. "And I'm sorry. I swear I am. Everybody with a TV knows you were kicked out of the league for drugs. And then that girl, whatever her name was. You so fucked up behind that, you still ain't ever told me her name."

"What does any of that have to do with me being in here?"

"I don't know. Nothing. But, I'm just saying, you been through so much, and I can't stand to see you ..." he paused, trying to organize words in his mind, "you know, cleaning up other people's yards."

"Nobody ever forced a pipe into my mouth. No one forced me to take that first hit, or any of the others." Jordan patted his chest. "I did this shit to my damn self. Jevon, how many times I gotta tell you that money don't make the man. Man makes money, and even then," he snapped his fingers, "just like that, it's gone. Covet it, praise it, and watch how fast you'll lose it." He couldn't help but think of all the wild cocaine parties, waking up in strange women's beds with no memories of the night before. "Have you ever thought that I might enjoy landscaping?"

"I just want more for you, for us. You've always been the one that made shit happen, and I've always been the fuck up."

"Still are."

Ignoring him, Jevon continued. "For once I just wanted to make shit happen for us."

"Fuck, Jevon! Fuck, fuck, fuck!" Jordan put the phone down, sat back in his chair, and put both hands over his face.

Nervous and scared, Jevon just sat there with the phone to his ear waiting for Jordan to pick the receiver back up.

A moment later Jordan grabbed the receiver from the hook on the gray partition wall. "So, what do you expect me to do, Jevon?"

"Nothing." He shook his head. "Nothing at all. For once in our lives, I'll make everything right."

"What's that supposed to mean?"

"Just what I said. You'll be a free man tomorrow." Jevon dropped the phone and got up before Jordan could say anything else.

Chapter 8

"**S**uicide!"

She nodded her head.

"But why? Why?" Jordan banged a fist against the visiting room glass. "I just saw Jevon yesterday." He looked up at the ceiling. "Lord, please tell me this wasn't what he was talking about before he left."

"If I wouldn't have walked into the apartment when I did, he'd be dead," Sunny said into the Dekalb County jail's visiting room phone receiver.

"This is crazy." Jordan shook his head. "I mean, it just doesn't make sense."

"Suicide never does."

"I know that, but you don't know my brother. He never leaves his car door, bedroom door, apartment door, nothing unlocked. When we were seven, in broad daylight, a man walked into the back door of our home and robbed and shot and killed our mother and father. Since then, Jevon has never left anything unlocked."

"I'm sorry," Sunny said.

"And you, I mean, do you make it a habit of walking into people's unlocked homes?"

"I knocked, and no one answered," she said.

"Does that mean—"

"Why are you giving me the third degree? If I hadn't walked into the apartment when I did, your brother would be dead."

"Look," he let out a deep breath, "I apologize. I just... I've just been through a lot these past couple days." He ran his fingers across his bald head.

She nodded her understanding.

"I just need to get outta here before I lose my damn mind."

"Can I do anything?"

"Do you have twenty-five hundred dollars?"

"For what?"

"This morning a paid attorney whom I'd never met or talked to, showed up and represented me at my bond hearing. Another thing that I'm confused about. Anyway, the judge ended up ordering my bail at twenty-five thousand dollars."

"Soooooo, you've got the other twenty one thousand?"

"It would be twenty-two five." He looked at her wondering what type of math she was doing. "And no, I don't have twenty-two thousand dollars. I don't need it. Ten percent of the bond figure is what I need to bond out."

"Oh... I see," she said.

"Sooo, do you have it?"

"Not on me."

This had to be the dumbest thing on two legs. He smiled. "Sunny, I wouldn't think you'd carry that much cash on you. What I meant was, do you have access to that type of cash?"

"Oh," she said, hitting herself with an open palm on her forehead, "silly me. Yeah, I have it in my bank account. I'll just go to Bank of Amer..." she put a hand over her mouth. She whispered, "I'm sorry. I didn't mean to mention the B-A-N-K word."

"Sunny." He closed his eyes. "There's nothing wrong with saying the word bank. Bank! Bank! Bank!" He shouted.

"Shhh," she put a finger over her mouth. Still whispering she said, "I heard prison phones are monitored."

He took a deep breath. "Sunny," he spoke slowly, "look at the white plastic cord connected to the phone." He paused. "Okay, now I want you to pull that cord."

The thick plastic phone cord connected to Jordan's receiver moved in the direction she pulled.

He smiled. "See?"

"See what?"

"Sunny, you're speaking through a plastic cord. There's no way for us to be monitored."

"Don't talk to me like I'm a retard, Jordan. I'm not stupid. I don't make it a habit of visiting prisons. How am I supposed to know the frigging phone is a fake?"

He wanted to say something, but he needed Sunny's money to make bond. Although they were only two minutes apart, Jordan had always looked after his older twin. And this time was no different. Jordan loved Jevon more than he loved himself, and more for Jevon's sake, he had to get out before Jevon made any more dumb moves.

"Again, I'm sorry, Sunny. I really need your help."

Still pouting, with her bottom lip stuck out, she asked, "What do you want me to do?"

"I need you to write something down."

She rummaged through her Coach bag and retrieved a tube of red lipstick and a piece of paper.

"Jennifer Green, 404-555-1010. She's an old friend." He thought back to the other times when his high school sweetheart's family came through for him when Jevon got arrested. "She owns *Free at Last bail bonds*."

"So, you want me to take her the money?"

"Please." He nodded his head. "But first, give her a call. The number I gave you is her cell." Before rising out of his seat, he said, "Sunny, you just don't know how much I appreciate this. He placed the receiver back in its cradle just as she signaled for him to pick it back up.

He sat back down and picked the phone up.

"Uhm, I forgot to mention."

"What?" he asked, trying not to show his frustration.

"I sort of took the letter before the ambulance got there."

"What letter?" he asked.

"The suicide letter, dingy."

Did this space cadet just call me dingy? "What suicide letter?"

She huffed. "The one Jevon wrote."

"What did it say?"

"It didn't say anything. Letters don't speak, silly." She laughed while pulling out the paper she wrote Jennifer's info on. "Darn!" With a sheepish look on her face, she said, "I must have left a tube of lipstick uncapped." She placed a wrinkled piece of paper smeared with red lipstick, to the glass partition.

Oh Lord, give me strength, he said to himself.

"Okay, okay," she said removing the paper from the window and sliding her chair closer to the glass. She looked up. "You ready?"

With his teeth clinched, he said, "Yes."

"Dear Jordan as you know everything I touch turns to shit. Since Mom and Dad passed, you've taken care of me. And now I had a one-shot chance of taking care of you, and I fucked it up. By the time you read this I'll be dead and you'll be a free man. I'm sorry for all the trouble I've been. This is my third strike and you know I'll get life. I'd rather be dead than live my life behind bars. I just want to let you know that I love you with all my heart. And remember, I did this for you.

Did what for me?

She continued reading. "I left all the evidence, prints, money, and bank bags under my bed in the apartment.

I love you. Twin, I'm so proud of the way you beat that crack monkey off your back. Jevon."

Chapter 9

"*W*hat?' Sunny asked after getting into Jevon's ten year old 635i sparkling black BMW.

"Whachu' mean, what?" he said before pulling out of the Dekalb County jail parking area.

"That look on your face. It's like I've done something."

"You did, at least I hope the hell you did," he said.

"Did what?"

"You have got be the dumbest thing walking. I mean seriously, how do you even get through an entire day by yourself? I mean really. How do you survive?"

"Since I can't read your frigging facial expressions I'm dumb? She took off her seat belt and turned toward him. "Obviously, you didn't think I was too dumb to go into the jail and make your brother think that you tried to kill yourself. I wasn't too dumb for you to trust me enough to slice your wrists this morning. How dumb was I this morning when I was sucking your dick and making you breakfast?"

"You damn near severed an artery. And I still got a bad taste in my mouth from those burnt up ass eggs you fried."

"I burnt your eggs because you wouldn't let me up until you came in my mouth," she said.

"Okay, Sunny, lets not argue." He pulled off into traffic. "Do you think he fell for it?"

"Fell for what?"

"The letter. The story," Jevon said.

"Yep. He was really sad. Jordan loves you so much, Jevon." She looked down at the BMW's immaculate gray carpeting. "I'm like my sister now. How could you do this to him?"

"Not you, too," he said shaking his head while pulling up to a street light. He turned toward her. "Look, my brother's strong. I hired a good lawyer for him. Hell, he'll be out before dark. Besides, Jordan's a soldier. He can do four, five years standing on his head if it comes to that; and with the recreational facilities in prison, he can get back into football-playing shape. By the time he gets out, I'll have flipped the quarter million twenty times over. Then, me and Jordan will be set for life, even if he doesn't play ball again."

"You mean the $125,000," Sunny said.

"Yeah, that's what I said."

"No, Jevon," she scolded. "You said the quarter million."

"Whatever, you know what I meant."

"I know what you said."

"Fuck, why does everything gotta be a got damn argument with you?" Not looking, Jevon pulled off into traffic. "Shit!" he screamed, while mashing on the brakes.

After hitting the back of the police car, the BMW went into a tail spin, hitting a van and then flipping over before a utility pole stopped the car from doing any more damage to oncoming traffic.

It was only by the grace of God that prevented the police officer and the van's driver from being seriously injured. Jevon and Sunny were a whole other story.

"Lord have mercy," one police officer said, shaking his head, while looking at the shattered windows and the crushed upside down BMW, wrapped around a utility pole.

Chapter 10

Sharon stormed into the private hospital room at Dekalb General. "You son of a bitch. You fucking son of a bitch," she cried.

Jevon hit the OFF button on the televisions remote control before hitting the *up* button on the hospital bed.

"You killed my baby, Jevon Hayes," she cried. "You killed my baby."

"I know you're hurt, and I'm truly sorry, but you have to calm down—"

"Calm down my ass!" She started hitting Jevon in the chest. "Calm down!" she repeated at a hysterical pitch.

He winced as a sharp pain shot through his chest. He grabbed her arms to stop the onslaught of blows. "Woman, is you crazy," he said, making eye contact. "I done already said that I'm sorry."

"Not as sorry as you're going to be Jevon Hayes."

"Sharon, it ain't like I intentionally hit a police car, hydroplaned, flipped my ride, and ran into a utility pole." Taking a calmer approach, he continued, "Look, if I could trade places with Sunny I would, but I—"

"Liar!" she shouted. "Let me go, she jerked away from his grasp. "You wouldn't trade places with God, if you were the one who killed him. You self-serving son of a bitch."

"What do you want me to do, Sharon?" He winced as a sharp pain began at his ribs and seemed to shoot to every nerve ending inside his body. Gritting his teeth, he continued. "There is nothing I can do, to bring your sister back. Nothing."

Sharon let out a maniacal laugh. "My sister? Asshole, Sunny was my daughter."

Jevon's eyes were saucers. "Say again."

"I had Sunny when I was thirteen."

"But I thought—"

A defiant look on her face she continued. "I know what you thought. My parents moved to Augusta, Georgia, from Des Moines, Iowa after I had the baby. They raised us as sisters. And, no, I wasn't raped.

He was truly sorry about Sunny, but better her than him, he thought. He just wished Sharon would leave him in peace. He really didn't care to hear her sob story. Right now, his thoughts were solely on the quarter million hidden under the spare wheel of the totaled out BMW that was sitting in some police impound yard.

Damn, I'm gon' miss that always-arguing, ignorant bitch. Shit, she gave some boss head. His nature began to rise under the white hospital sheet.

Sharon looked up at Jevon. His lifeless eyes were focused on the black TV screen on the wall above his bed. "Jevon?"

Bitch been a freak all her damn life. I can't get no player points for bangin' momma and daughter. If I could, I'd go down in the player/pimp hall of fame.

"Jevon?" she called out again.

"Huh?"

"You truly are an insensitive bastard." Sharon stood beside the hospital bed, murder in her red eyes, trembling mad, her arms crossed.

He turned his head.

"Fuck you! Fuck you, Jevon! You don't give a shit about me or my daughter. You don't give a damn about anyone but Jevon Hayes."

"What the fuck are you talkin' about, Sharon?"

"Fuck you!"

"What do you want from me, Sharon? Two days ago, I banged my ribs up, and suffered a concussion in a car accident. My brother is probably losing his mind, sitting in a prison cell—"

"No thanks to you," she said.

"What's that supposed to mean?"

"You know damn well what it means, Jevon."

"That bitch can't keep... I'm sorry. I didn't mean—"

"Bitch!" she cried, throwing her hands in the air. "If my daughter wouldn't have gone into that jail for you she'd be here right now. And you have the audacity to call her a bitch."

He knew he'd messed up as soon as the word left his lips.

"You're the bitch." She pointed to Jevon.

He winced as he attempted to swing a leg over the side of the bed.

"What kind of man sets his brother up and then tips the police off to where he's at? I'll tell you what kind of man. A bitch of a man."

He closed his eyes and gritted his teeth as a million needles stabbed his body from the inside out as he put his weight on his legs, attempting to stand. "I don't know who you think you talkin' to, but I ain't the one."

"You'll be—"

"Shut the fuck up and let me speak." The pain was excruciating, but Jevon had to bear it to get his point across. "With the polygraph test you and all the bank employees had to take, the heat from the media, and whatever other unforeseen bullshit that came up, I did what I felt I had to do to protect me, Sunny, and your ungrateful ass."

Sharon walked to the door and opened it. "You no longer have to worry about my ungrateful ass!" she shouted at the top of her lungs. "You need to worry about protecting your own ass. The men in prison are going to love them pretty hazel eyes of yours."

"What? Where do you think you goin'?"

With her back to him, she said, "To hell if I don't pray, but before I go you'll be doing time for bank robbery, you bastard."

"You forgot about your part in all this," he said to her back.

With her hand on the door handle, she turned and smiled looking him in the eye. "I'm an innocent little ole Georgia white girl who was blackmailed by a big black man with a criminal background. I'm sure the D.A. will cut me a sweet deal in light of those circumstances."

Chapter 11

*J*evon's eyes were on the hospital room window, seemingly focused on the setting summer sun. But his mind was swimming through the dark, murky waters of indecision. Would Sharon go through with her threat? Worse, would Jordan find out about the set-up? A slew of thoughts ran through his mind as he lay on the hospital bed.

He looked at the beige hospital phone receiver he'd held for the past five minutes. Desperate, not knowing what to do or whom to call, he dialed the number of the only person he could possibly turn to.

He picked up on the third ring.

"CW, where you at, big dog?"

"Jevon?"

"Yeah, I'm sorry, bruh, but I have an emergency situation on my hands and I don't have anyone else to turn to."

The other end of the phone was silent.

"CW?"

"Sorry, I had to put the phone on mute. I'm walking outside Sugar's apartment."

"You messing with that stripper again?"

"Former stripper," the bishop corrected. "And I can't help it. The woman is walking crack, even with her drama."

"Does she know about your new wife?"

"I just told her."

"And?" Jevon asked.

"She tried to act ugly, until I reminded her of the $4,000 monthly allowance I give her. Without my money she'd still be stripping and she wouldn't be back in school."

"Oh," Jevon said.

"So, what's going on with you, Brother Hayes?"

"I need to tell you in person. I'm in Room 505 at Dekalb General Hospital."

"Dekalb General?"

"Long story, I'll explain when I see you. But right now I'm in a life-and-death situation."

"I'll be there after church tomorrow eve—"

"That'll be too late. CW," he pleaded, "this has everything to do with the quarter-mil, I'm investing in your Conyers Center City Mall development project."

*****

An hour later, slim, charismatic, sharp-dressing, popular Bishop CW Wiley was sitting at Jevon's bedside, legs crossed, admiring his manicured fingernails, as he listened to Jevon's story.

"Come on, bruh, don't look at me like that," Jevon pleaded. "I know what I did is real fu— messed up, but I did it for mine and Jordan's future."

"Jevon?"

"What? You don't believe me? You think I'd set my own twin up."

"It isn't about what I believe Jevon; it's about the truth. Now, I'm not gon' preach a sermon. What's done is done. Now we have to figure out what to do about this Sharon person."

"So, you're gon' help me?" Jevon asked, wincing as he sat up in bed. The look CW gave him made Jevon uncomfortable.

"Depends?" CW replied.

"On what?"

"Depends on how far you are willing to go to make this problem disappear," he said.

"Anything, I'll do anything." Tears of defeat cascaded down Jevon's face. "I'll get you the money in a couple days," Jevon said, unable to picture giving up all that money.

CW got up and propped a chair under the hospital room door lever.

"What are you doing?"

"Were you serious about doing anything?" CW asked.

"Look, I got the money tucked away in a safe place. I get outta here day after tomorrow and I swear it's yours. I can even tell you where it is, but you won't be able to—"

"I didn't say anything about any money," CW said as he stood next to Jevon's bed.

Nervous, not knowing what to think, Jevon asked, "Well, what do you want?"

CW unbuckled his pants.

"Oh hell nah. Hell double mothafucking nah." Jevon slapped himself in the chest, forgetting about his bandaged, bruised ribs. "Ahh," he gasped as several sharp pains shot through his body. Slowly, Jevon said, "All the pussy you get?"

"I want more," CW said, sticking his hand down his pants. "I need more."

"Dog, you be up in more pussy than an OB/GYN. How you gon' be a down-low preacher?"

He took his hand out, buttoned his slacks, and turned to the door. "Jevon, I'm not a punk, fag, sissy, or any of the derogatory names used to describe one who enjoys loving both male and female. And I'm definitely not on any down low. I thought I was your pastor and your friend," he took a couple steps, lifted the curtain and turned to face Jevon, "but now I see."

"Do you want the money or not?" Jevon asked.

CW turned back to the door, smiling at the sweet sound of fear resonating from Jevon's tone. CW shook his head, "No," he said with finality.

"So, that's it?" Jevon asked.

"It's what you want it to be," CW said, his back still to Jevon. His nature rising at every octave rise in Jevon's plea.

"How do I know you won't fuck me after I give you what you want?" Jevon asked.

CW shrugged. "You don't."

Chapter 12

"*J*ack, you know good and got damn well I ain't no shit sticker, but that nigger," Deputy Greenley pointed at Jordan, "got a mule dick if I ever seened one," Deputy Greenley said to the younger officer standing at the door.

"You get off looking at black men's dicks?" Jordan said as he spread his butt cheeks, bent over, and coughed.

"Boy, you ain't in no position to question me, especially with me holding this here night stick," he said, hitting the large black stick against the palm of his hand. "Does Abner Louima ring a bell?" Greenley asked.

Jordan rose up and flexed his neck muscles. With his back to the deputies, he replied, "Act like I'm Abner and watch how fast you swallow that stick."

"Are you threatening an officer of the law, boy?"

"No, that's illegal." He shrugged his shoulders. "I'm stating a fact."

"Don't get mad at me. I ain't the one on the way to SEG for ripping the phone off the wall."

"What did you expect?" Jordan shook his head. "I just found out my brother was in a serious car accident. I'm his only family. He could be dying as we speak."

"Well, I damn sure hope so. Nigger should've been the one that died instead of that white woman. You jigs don't get enough. Your women don't want you so you come at ours." Greenley hawked and spat some tobacco out of his mouth.

Jordan flinched after feeling the glob of sticky, wet tobacco on his left butt cheek. Suddenly, everything Jordan saw was a bright red. Before anyone knew it, Jordan was throwing a barrage of elbows and fists at the unsuspecting Deputy Greenley. He'd hit the man at least ten times before the other deputy jumped on Jordan's back and draped his nightstick around Jordan's neck. While choking and backpeddling, Jordan began to lose his balance. He swayed from left to right, dizzy for lack of oxygen. A minute later, his legs gave out and he crashed to the concrete cell floor, sending the deputy on his back crashing into the stainless steel lip of the toilet bowl.

Chapter 13

"*W*ho?" Jevon shouted after flushing the toilet and heading to answer the front door. He'd been home from the hospital a couple of hours now. His body was still sore, but the flexoril and percosets he was taking helped mask the pain.

Okay, relax girl. You've thought about this moment for two weeks. The man is all you can think about at home, at work in the Institution, and especially at group on Thursday nights. She breathed before nervously answering. "It's Dr. Jamison, Dr. Cheyenne Jamison."

Jevon opened the apartment door. "Yes, can I help you?"

Her heart melted. In his arms is the only place she wanted to be. "Jordan?"

Damn, good Lord, this woman had a body. He smiled. "Oh, yeah. Hi...Uhm... Ms. Jamison."

She had a confused look on her face as she asked, "I'm sorry, did I catch you at a bad time?"

"No. No. Come on in," Jevon said, walking gingerly toward the black leather couch that faced the 50-inch plasma TV that hung over the apartment fireplace. "Have a seat," he said changing directions and walking toward the kitchen. "Can I get you something to drink?"

"No, I'm fine," she said a little leery, before sitting down on the leather couch. The place was exceptionally clean, she thought as she looked around the nicely furnished black and white apartment.

A minute later he reached into his pants pocket and took a couple pills out and washed them down with a bottle of Corona before re-entering the living room and sitting down on the black lounge chair adjacent to the couch she sat on.

"I thought you didn't drink," she said.

"I don't," he said, taking another sip. "I mean, not really. I just sip from time to time to take the edge off of a rough day. This beer," he held it up in the air, "This'll last me a week."

An uncomfortable moment of silence passed between them, before she said, "I'm sorry, I don't usually do this."

"Do what?"

"Just pop up at a man's house without calling. It's just that I was worried when you didn't call or show up for group, so I got your address from the register you signed a couple weeks ago." She looked down and removed an invisible piece of lint from her cream-colored business skirt. "Like I said, I've never done anything like this, but I'm just, I'm just going to come right out and say it." She sighed. "I've thought about you every minute, every hour, every day for sixteen days. I even prayed that you'd come back to NA. Jordan, I've been practicing psychiatry for six years, and in that time I've seen and heard a lot."

Psychiatrist! Shit, baby bruh hit the money motherload. And the bitch was fine, and refined.

"But I've never been moved like you moved me. At first I thought it was a passing phase. A lonely woman's crush. No offense, but I've worked to hard and too long to get to where I am today"

Jevon nodded, wondering what the hell she was talking about.

"What I mean is," she let out a deep breath. "I'm a doctor and this is just crazy insane, that I am feeling like this, acting so out of character, all because of a one night meeting with a handsome man, who happens to be a recovering addict. I mean, Jordan, am I going through some type of crisis? Is this a crush?" She got up and took two steps and reached for his hand. She shook her head from sided to side. "It's not a crush, is it Jordan?"

Oh, she gone. Jordan done really put a superman mack game down on this one. He shook his head. Looking into her watery big brown eyes, Jevon said, "No, it's not. I knew we were meant to be, the day I laid eyes on you."

"You mean night," she corrected.

"Ms. James—"

"Jamison, Cheyenne Jamison." She looked at Jevon with a quizzical look on her face. "Is everything okay?" she asked.

"No, everything's not, *okay*." He sighed. He searched his mind for something to say. He couldn't tell her about the car accident, because of Sunny. He'd sent Sunny to those NA meetings to snare Jordan. She only went two times, but he couldn't take a chance on that being two times too many. An idea came to mind. He said, "You probably heard about it on TV."

"Heard about what?"

"Well, eight days ago, on Friday, I saw a woman being abducted. I chased the car she was ushered into for maybe five, six miles. Long story short, the passenger started shooting; I put my foot on the gas pedal of my Porsche and slammed into the Cadillac, they were driving." He paused. "Cheyenne, I have very little memory of that night. I just got out of the hospital today. If it weren't for the abducted woman's testimony, I still wouldn't have known what happened that night."

"Oh Lord, you must've had some sort of head injury," she said, remembering that he drove a Toyota Corolla, and not a Porsche.

"Besides two fractured ribs and a lot of bruising, the doctors had to induce a coma."

"You had brain swelling?" she said.

He nodded.

"Oh, my God." She put a hand over her mouth. "I had no idea."

"I know. Newspaper and magazine reporters have requested multiple interviews, but out of respect for the victim's privacy and me not wanting to be in the limelight, I refused." The words came out before he had time to think. He braced himself for her reaction to his bullshit transparent lie.

"Jordan Hayes," she reached out and grabbed his hands, "where have you been all my life?"

Caught off guard he said, "What, uhm, looking for you." It came out more as a question than a statement.

He could not believe that she was really a psychiatrist. She was supposed to be trained to detect bullshit.

In no time, he was sitting on the couch, her body in his arms.

The kiss was long and passionate. He still could not believe his luck. Something was definitely not right with this woman, but he decided to go as far as his game took him.

With expert skill, using one hand, his fingers went up her blouse and walked up the middle of her back and undid her bra. He planted mini tongue kisses on the back of her ear, and down the side of her neck.

"Oh yeah," she said.

He stopped at her shoulders. There, he licked and sucked on her tense muscles, giving her an erotic tongue massage unlike anything she'd ever imagined.

"Ohhhh, Ohhh, Jor-Jordan," she cooed.

Caught up in the moment, she ran her fingers up and around his bald head and down the back of his neck. Slowly and in pain he maneuvered his body off of the couch and onto the floor. Now, on his knees, he gently pushed her head back onto the couch. Never breaking eye contact, he grabbed hold of one Dolce & Gabana heeled sandal, removed it, and began massaging her feet and toes, ignoring the pain that began to overpower the little blue and white pills he'd swallowed.

While removing the other sandal, he sent jolts of intense pleasure up her spine after he put part of her foot inside of his mouth. His tongue darted and stabbed erogenous zones she didn't even realize she had.

She threw her head back. "What are you doing to me Jordan Hayes?"

"Everything you want and need," he replied while removing her panties from under her skirt.

She continued massaging his scalp.

"Oh, Oh Jordan. I can't be-be-believe I'm doing this. I should-We shouldn't be..."

His wet tongue made like a jack hammer, tapping away at her swollen pinkish clit. Veins in her forehead were visibly breathing as she strained to stop the tsunami of juices threatening to explode from the inner depths of her pleasure zone.

"We shouldn't be... Oh, oh..." She grabbed his head with both hands. Her legs began to tremble. "I-I can't take... Jordan, oh Jordan! Shit!" She screamed at the top of her lungs as a volcano of ecstasy erupted inside of her. "Stop it, Jordan. Please," she cried. She tried to move away from his magical fingers, lips, and tongue, but the grip he had on her was paralyzing.

He continued using two fingers as a clit crimp while his tongue darted, danced, and massaged her clit and the inner walls of her love tunnel.

"I-I can't stop cumming. Make it stop, Jordan. Make it stop."

He used one hand to unbutton and unzip his white linen shorts while his face twisted and turned between her butter pecan-colored legs.

He thought about pulling a condom out of his wallet. But on second thought he decided not to. After what had happened between him and the bishop, he needed to feel like a man. And what better way than to make a baby. And who better to give his seed to; she was a medical doctor, young, fine, and she had to pull well into six figures.

"Condom, you got one?" she asked as he held her legs behind her head, the swollen tip of his manhood teasing the opening of her love nest.

"Jordan?" She was about to ask again when he plunged himself into her pool of warm wetness.

"Ughhh," she gasped. Almost instantly, she came for the eighth time in thirty minutes.

"Who's your daddy, girl?" he asked, sliding all eight-point-three inches of his tree-trunk thick manhood in and out of her.

"You are. Thank you, God. Thank you so much," she cried, tears running down her face. "I'm yours. I'm all yours, Jordan Hayes. Don't hurt me. Please, Jordan, don't-don't hurt me."

"Never that. I got you boo." He smiled. Proud that he'd put on his all-time greatest sexual and acting performance. "Now, tell Daddy whose pussy this is."

"Yours! Yours! Yours!" she screamed.

"No matter what you do, baby, don't ever give this pussy to another soul. Don't even dream about another dick up in mine," he said.

She shook her head before grabbing the sides of his face and looking him in his hazel eyes. "Never. I swear to you, Jordan Hayes, I'm yours as long as you want me. Just don't lie to me. I can handle anything but lies."

Chapter 14

"Lies, man. Lies." Jordan slammed a fist down on the metal table. "That cracker threatened to sodomize me with a nightstick." Appealing to his brother from behind the Plexiglas visiting room wall, he continued. "He spit tobacco on my ass, Jevon. I lost it, man, I just lost it."

For the first time in two weeks, Jevon was finally allowed to see Jordan, who'd been on disciplinary lockdown.

"I'm sorry," Jevon said.

"Man, this has been two weeks of pure hell." Jordan looked up. "Jevon, you know I love you more than I love myself, don't you?"

Feeling just a little queasy about his betrayal, he replied, "Yes. I do."

"I would serve ten life sentences before I'd let anything happen to you."

"I know you would, and you know I'd do the same for you."

"I know you would, Jevon, truly, I do. But I need you to be straight up with me. Can you at least do that?" Jordan asked.

Jevon nodded his head, knowing damn well he couldn't explain Sunny being in the car with him when he was supposed to be in the hospital, being treated for attempted suicide.

"Did you try to take your life for the second time in a 24 hour period?"

Confused, Jevon said, "Huh?"

"The car accident. Was it really an accident?"

"Yes, I mean, no. Uhm, Sunny called me right after she left you. She told me what she told you, and I flipped out. I got up and left the hospital right then and there."

Remembering what Cherry once told him about hospitals and suicide attempts, Jordan said, "I thought hospitals kept you for at least twenty-four hours for surveillance after a suicide attempt."

"They do. But I didn't ask to leave, I just left. I still can't believe Sunny came down and actually told you that I tried to kill myself."

"You did, didn't you?"

He dropped his head to his chest, feeling terrible about the lies he was telling Jordan. "Yeah, but that's not the point. What I do to myself is my bus—"

"No, it's our business. You're my only brother, my only everything." Jordan put a hand over his chest. "Jevon, you're my heart. If something happened to you, at this point in my life I don't know what I would do. Since Momma and Daddy died, haven't I taken care of you? Haven't I always had your back?"

Jevon nodded.

"So, why didn't you tell me about the three strikes?"

"She told you that, too?"

"She read the note to me, Jevon. And she shouldn't have had to tell me. Why didn't you tell me? Don't you know I would've taken the fall for you? That was some stupid shit you did with that bank, but I would never let you do life behind that dumb shit."

"Jordan, I couldn't let you do that."

"*Let!* You ain't lettin' me do shit. You're my brother, and I love you." Switching gears back to where the conversation began, Jordan asked, "You never answered my question."

"What question?"

"The car accident."

"Man, I just said fuck it. It was a spur of the moment decision. I was at a light about to turn into the county jail complex. I was coming to say good-bye, and explain why I was gon' take my life. And it dawned on me that if I told you, you'd find a way to talk me out of it. So I just said fuck it and hit the gas."

"Damn, Jevon!" He stood up. "What the fuck were you thinking?"

"Hayes!" an officer shouted.

Jordan slowly sat back down in the silver metal visiting room folding chair.

"I wasn't thinking."

"You killed an innocent woman. Now, you have to live with that for the rest of your life. Selfish. Fucking selfish. Fuck, Jevon, that woman will never see—"

"Jordan, I know! I know!" he cried. His brother had always been able to make him feel lower than the dirt he walked on. Ever since their parents died, Jordan got a perverse kick out of making him feel like he was less than worthless.

72

"Did you at least apologize to the girl's family?"

"I could only find her sister. And by the time I got to her apartment, the door was barricaded with yellow crime scene tape," Jevon said, hoping Jordan hadn't seen or heard the story on TV.

"What happened there?"

"Sunny's sister, Sharon, succeeded where I didn't," he mumbled under his breath.

"Speak up, man."

"She shot herself in the head," Jevon shouted, forgetting where he was, but not forgetting the price he'd paid to have Sharon killed.

"Keep it down, Booth 6," a visiting room officer shouted.

Jordan just shook his head, thinking of all the trouble Jevon had caused.

"Don't look at me like that. Man, I know I fucked up. I mean, what did you expect? I'm a fuck-up. That's what I am. That's what I do—"

"It's what you *did*. You were a fuck up. I ain't gon' sugarcoat, shit. It was what it was, but now I'm givin' you a chance to change."

"Change what?" Jevon interrupted.

Jordan reached out from behind the Plexiglas. "Your life. Man, look, if I can stop using, then you can change." He tapped his temple with his index finger. "Think, Jevon, you have to start thinking and being more considerate to others."

"Man, I need a drink," Jevon blurted out, hoping to get out of there before Jordan put him and Sunny together. It was obvious, since the car accident occurred less than fifteen minutes after Sunny walked out of the jail visiting room.

"No, you need to use some of that bank money and pay Longfellow the rest of the retainer for my defense."

"Whachu mean?" Jevon asked.

"I mean what you think I mean," Jordan said. "In exchange for the assault charges being dropped, I plead to one count of unarmed robbery and I'll be home in February, of 09."

"That's damn near five years away."

"Four years, six months, and thirteen days, counting the sixteen days I've already served."

"What about bond?" Jevon asked, knowing it had already been revoked.

"I messed that up when I caught the assault charge."

Trying his best to hide his excitement and relief, Jevon said, "Don't worry, Jordan, don't' worry about shit. When you get out, you won't ever have to work another day in your life."

"Come on, Jevon, no more schemes. Can't you just do right for once?"

Jevon shook his head and got up. He was about to hang the phone receiver up when Jordan said, "Wait!"

Nothing Jordan said could ruin the mood that he was trying his best to mask. It didn't matter if Jordan assumed he was going to do something stupid. He'd show him. He'd show the world what Jevon Hayes was capable of.

Placing the receiver back to his ear, Jevon asked, "What now?"

"Earlier that night, before I was arrested, I met a woman. No, I met the very reason for my existence."

"Come on, dog, chill with that poetic shit," Jevon said, sitting back down.

"No, Jevon, I'm dead serious." Jevon watched his brother's eyes light up. "I can't quite explain it. Her name is Dr. Cheyenne Jamison. And as long as I can communicate with her, I'll be just fine." He smiled. "I need you to look under my Drakkar cologne on top of my dresser. Her number is written on a piece of paper. I got my phone restriction lifted today. I'll call you tonight for the number. Jevon, I can't wait for you to meet her."

Shit, I just fucked the reason for my brother's existence. "Jordan, you always tell me to think before I leap. Now who's not thinking?"

"Say what?"

"Come on, bruh. You say you really feel this broad, right?"

"Without a doubt."

"So why burden her with this? I mean, I bet she has feelings for you, too, but it's not fair for her to do time with you. Let's keep it real. Look at you, dude. You a recovering addict without a pot to piss in. And what's her name, Cheyenne? Dog, she's a psychiatrist, no doubt, balling and playing with lawyers, and doctor-type niggas. What she gotta gain by coming to see you every weekend for damn near five years? You think she gon' let that pussy starve for that long?"

"How'd you know she was a psychiatrist?"

"Come on, dog, you just told me."

"No." Jordan shook his head. "I said she was a doctor, I never said what kind."

Shit.

"Jevon?"

"All right, All right man. Long story short, I went through your room. I called the number. Don't ask why, I don't know. I was suicidal. I was thinking all types of crazy shit. Anyway, a woman picked up. I didn't say who I was, but she introduced herself and I hung up."

75

Although the story sounded fishy, Jordan was too caught up in the possibility of not ever hearing her Sade-like voice again, not seeing the way she toyed with her ring finger when she was nervous, or not being able to enjoy the performance her left dimple put on when she laughed.

"You're right, Jevon. It's not gon' be easy, but you're right. Hell, I don't deserve Cheyenne after what I let happen to Cherry."

Jevon hadn't heard a word his brother had just said. He could hardly believe his luck. The car accident was actually the best thing that had ever happened to him. Sunny died, CW handled Sharon, Jordan caught an assault charge and took the bank robbery rap, and he had some million-dollar pussy on his team.

Chapter 15

" $\mathcal{K}$ iss my black ass!"
"Come again, Ms. Sharell?" the burly female
hospital PA asked while she was standing outside Cherry's-
six by-nine room.

"Is it the kiss, the my, or the ass? Which one do you not
understand, you big Godzilla-lookin' boo-goblin?" Cherry
said while sitting on her bunk in the maximum security unit
of the Georgia Regional Mental Institution. Her girlfriend,
Karen continued painting Cherry's nails as if nothing was
going on.

"Do I call you out of your name, Ms. Sharell? No, I
don't, so I'd appreciate it if you didn't call me out of
mine."

Cherry looked up to her right where Ms. Joiner stood
outside the steel door. "I'm sorry, Oom-foo-foo. I'll try to
refrain from calling you boo-zilla, or mo-ugly, or any of the
other names that fit you so well, but it's hard when you
keep fucking with me. KP been doin' my nails for the past
three years, every Tuesday, at one; and at least every other

Tuesday you come fuckin' with me in the midst of her hookin' my shit up."

"Hmmm, let's see," Ms. Joiner put a finger to the side of her face, "you've had, what, zero visits in three years, and I think you're getting out, hmm, when was that?" She wiggled a finger toward Cherry. "Oh yeah," she snapped her pudgy fingers, "that's right, the day after never. So, I think you have all the time in the world to get your crusty nails done."

"Sasquatch, you just mad 'cause I'm locked up in here and we both get the same amount of dick." Cherry pointed to the PA's white curtain-sized dress. "If you lose four of those asses attached to your hurricane hips and give birth to that elephant threatening to pop out your fat-ass belly, then you might just be able to pay a blind man to hit that cobweb, desert drought dry pussy of yours."

The two guards accompanying Ms. Joiner snickered.

"One of these days... One of these days," Ms. Joiner said balling and unballing her large fists.

"One of these days what, bitch?" Cherry snatched her hand away from Karen, stood up and shouted, "Boo," before jumping toward the taller, much heavier, forty-something-looking, Physicians Assistant.

Although, Cherry was at least three feet away from the door, which the PA stood outside of, she still jumped back. But the two medium-built hospital guards didn't. They rushed in and reached out and grabbed Cherry. "Let me go," she shouted, twisting and turning until breaking away from one of the men.

"What the—" The guard she broke away from, grabbed the side of his face.

Cherry continued swinging, looking like a cross between a wild woman and a female prize fighter. It took nearly three minutes before the guards got her under control.

"Oh yeah, daddy," she panted. "You feel like a man now that you have all 130 pounds of me in a chokehold?"

"What's goin' on here?" Dr. Jamison walked up. "You two let her go."

"She scratched me," the guard holding the side of his face said.

"Let her go, now, Officer Burrows!"

"But—"

"I saw and heard everything." Dr. Jamison said. Turning her attention to Ms. Joiner, she asked, "Do you need to administer any medication to Ms. Sharell, or Ms. Parker?" She pointed to Cherry and Karen.

"No, ma'am."

"Did Ms. Sharell call for you?"

"No, ma'am."

"Well, why are you bothering them?"

"Look, Ms. Jamison—"

"Dr. Jamison," Cheyenne corrected. "Furthermore, the only thing I am about to look at, is you walking out of this unit."

Ms. Joiner made a sucking sound as she turned and left with the two guards in tow.

Ten minutes later, Karen was gone and Cheyenne and Cherry sat at the foot of the cell's twin bed.

"Dr. Jamison, you are a real stand-up lady. I don't know why you do it, but I'm just glad you do."

"Do what?" Cheyenne asked.

"Alienate yourself from the staff. You seem to always be standin' up for one of us girls," Cherry said.

"Cheryl, do you know the difference between the women committed to this institution and me?"

"How much time you got?" Cherry asked.

"I'm serious."

"So am I," Cherry said.

"Let me tell you the difference. You and all the lost queens in this maximum-security, God-forsaken hell, have either a chemical imbalance set off by God knows what, or the world has become too much and you all have crawled into an invisible shell," Cheyenne put a comforting arm around Cherry's shoulder, "one, I'm trying to crack."

After three years at Georgia Regional, Cherry still found it hard to digest that Dr. Jamison was so real. Time and again she stood up against staff or institution policy if it violated an inmate's human rights. For this, Dr. Jamison was widely disliked by most prison hospital staff. The only reason she hadn't been transferred was because the current administration was afraid that the inmates would riot and attempt to burn the institution down like they'd tried last time they attempted to transfer the doctor.

"Girl, at any given time I could be in a blue suit, here with you. Or, worse, in a padded cell with a white jacket on. And then I'd want someone who cared to look out for my best interest. After all, we're all in here to get better."

"Nah, Doc, you mean," Cherry pointed to herself, "*we're* in here to get better."

"No, Cheryl, I mean exactly what I said. You got to be a little cuckoo to work here, don't you think?"

They shared a rare moment of patient-doctor laughter. A moment that made Cheyenne's job worth the one-hour commute, four times a week, ten hours a day.

"Doc?" Cherry turned and looked up at Cheyenne. "You think they'll ever let me out?"

She nodded. "Yes, I know they will. And if they don't, I'm sure you'll find a way to escape again."

"Nah, Doc, I'm through running. I just wanna be free from this... this, what do you call it, erotogenic masochism." She diverted her eyes from Cheyenne. "I hate to say it, but I sort of provoked Ms. Joiner and the guards, hoping they'd attack me." She began to cry. "What is wrong with me, Doc? Why am I like this? Why do I get so turned on when I'm causing someone intense pain, or vice-versa."

"I don't know," she said hugging Cherry, "but together we're gon' beat this thing."

"Doc?" Cherry began to cry. "I'm not really a bad person."

"I know. I know you're not," she consoled the beautiful young Hershey dark chocolate woman.

"They were all mean. Abusive. I only did what the law wouldn't do. I never cut off a dick, a penis that didn't deserve it. Women all over the world are raped and beaten hourly, and most of the abusers go unpunished. I swear, Doc, I ain't ever hurt a man that didn't hurt me or another sister first."

"Cheryl, we've been over this, time and again. We have to find a way to suppress those urges. I have evil thoughts, but I don't act on them. We have to learn to be patient and let God do His job.

"I know, Doc." She nodded. "You're right."

"Just look at how far you've come in three years. When you first got here you were a wild woman, provoking staff and inmates making them attack, and when they did you would become so aroused... well you know the rest."

She looked up and wiped her tears with the back of her hand. "I was out there for real, huh, Doc?"

"Yes, you were. But look at you now. You even forgave the women who left that scar on your face and the ones on your arm."

"Yeah, that was easy; they were defending themselves, sort of. I can't stay mad at that. Hell, I would've done the same if the shoe was on the other foot."

Cherry never mentioned the man smoking crack sitting in a corner of the hotel suite watching while the women attacked and maimed her. She didn't blame the women for her knife marks, or the beating that had caused her to miscarry. Jordan may have been ignorant to the fact that she had been carrying his baby, but in Cherry's eyes that will never excuse him for sitting at the edge of a hotel bed smoking crack, watching as two girls stabbed and beat her.

She would just bide her time. Every night for the past three years, Cherry masturbated thinking about ways to make Jordan Hayes hurt. There were hundreds of thousands of ways to hurt, and her mind never ran out of ways to make him suffer.

TWISTED FATE
Part II

you'd have to be me
to see me
feel me
to free me
until then, call me crazy
for I'm invisible
to the sane eye
because the sane eye can't see
for it's the sane who suffer from
true insanity
so because they don't see me
they cage my body
but every night I take a leap
escaping through your dreams
I stalk and creep
using my surgeon's blade
as a mirror to your soul
seeking out the sins
you commit
against little girls
young and old
when I find you
and trust and believe
find you, I will
Cherry's the name
and I'll come dressed
and more than ready to kill
the hopes and dreams of the insane-sane
I'll even let you watch me cum
while you die in pain
rob the essence of my sister
if you dare
and I'll slice it off
without a thought or care

Chapter 16

*O*ver four and a half years had passed. The year was 2009. Suicide was at an all time high. Over the last two years the nation's homeless population had doubled. The dollar had fallen to an all time low. Banks everywhere had closed their doors. Major car manufacturers all over the nation had closed several plants. The country was in a time of turmoil like it hadn't seen since the stock market crash of 1929. Despite all of this. Despite Georgia's ranking as the number two state for joblessness, Jevon Hayes had done very well off of other peoples misery.

He'd used his wife's money and false promises to swindle desperate people out of their homes. Once he'd acquired them for as low as twenty cents on the dollar, he either resold them to other investors, or cleaned them up and rented them out.

Two months ago, back in February with nothing but the wind in his pockets Jordan had re-entered society, even more disappointed in his brother then he had been when he found out that he'd robbed a bank.

Wild Cherry

It was early, around five. People were still getting off work and fighting that crazy Friday Atlanta rush-hour traffic. It was unseasonably hot for April. The sun was smiling. Leaves danced with the wind. Even traffic moved at a slow steady pace, which was unusual for the Atlanta Friday stop and go-stand still highways.

Life was beautiful. Jevon Hayes had a successful wife, a beautiful three-year-old daughter, and he'd just flim-flammed another wanna-be real estate investor at the 41st annual luncheon commemorating the death of Dr. Martin Luther King Jr. And best of all he'd convince Jordan to go out with him tonight, so he could take a crack at Bishop Wiley's wife, that fine ass Monica.

"Whachu gon' do, dog?" Jevon asked.

"I can't hear you." Jordan said.

"Hold on," he said, using the hands free cell phone system that came with the new SL 500 Benz he'd recently bought. "Let me roll the windows up." A second later, Jevon asked, "Can you hear me now?"

"Yep."

"So, what's up, you ready to go ho' shoppin?"

"Sorry, bro, I'm gon' have to pass."

"Man, what's up wit' you? One of them booty bandits get to you when you was on lock?"

"Don't even joke with me like that. You know I don't play those types of games."

"I'm just sayin', you been out damn near two months, and you ain't kicked it with your twin. Hell, you ain't even popped your freedom cherry."

"Jevon, you know I'm a changed man. The kings I left behind in prison raised me, and if it—"

Jevon interrupted, "weren't for them and all the books you read, you would still be asleep, yeah, yeah, yeah, I know."

"You need to come down and hang out with me for a day at the Boys Club, Mr. I-Know. You'll see for yourself how bad these kids need positive black men in their lives. These kids will inspire you to wanna do right."

"Look, you do your right and I'll do mine, and we can live happily the hell ever after."

"It ain't about you, Jevon. It's about making a positive difference in the lives of our youth. A lot of somebodyies helped shape and mold us into who we are; that's why we have to get involved. That's why we have to help them shape their futures."

"Only thing I have to help shape is my wallet. Besides, you ain't gon' change the world trying to impact the lives of a handful of bad-ass kids."

"One of my boys *will* become the next Barack Obama, Malcolm X, or Dr. King." Jordan paused. "Man, you have to wake up."

"No the hell I don't. I'm just fine sleeping my life away. Matter of fact, I'm gon' sleep my way to the bank, and into some new pussy tonight."

Jordan winced. He hated the way his brother treated his wife. The woman he, himself should've married.

"You still haven't seen my championship ring?" Jordan asked. "The kids would love to see it."

"Nah, man. You sure you didn't pawn it back in your get-high days?"

"No. That ring is-was the only thing I had left from my NFL days."

Angry that his plan to use Jordan to woo the Bishop's wife was quickly disintegrating, he barked. "I ain't seen it," Jevon said.

"Anyway, back to what I was saying."

"Do I have to hear this?" Jevon asked.

"Yes, you do. Now, look." He paused, thinking of Cheyenne and his beautiful three-year-old hazel-eyed niece. "There's so much more to life than sex and money—"

"Call me simple, then, 'cause I'm happy living in Pussy Paradise. Hell, come to think of it, I am making a difference. Shit, with the seventeen to one men-to-women ratio in the ATL, and all the booty bandits running around, somebody got to serve these ho's. I'm filling the dick deficiency void in the black community. They say love makes the world go round. I'm just trying to do my share."

"Jevon, you think everything's a joke. You just don't get it, do you?"

"Ah, nigga, miss me with all that. Five years ago, you was getting' high and running up in any ho' that spread her legs."

"*Six* years ago." Jordan corrected him. "I'd been clean for nine months before I went in, and Sunny was the only." He paused. "Anyway, that was then."

"Okay, look." Jevon decided to try another tactic to get his twin to go out with him. "Just for old times, let's do recruitment Fridays, like we used to. Hell, I'll even throw you a thousand dollars if you come up stronger than me. You used to be the man, in your day, but Jevon Hayes is the new and improved Hayes Ho Gigolo. Since you rusty and shit, I'll even snag you a piece of microwave pussy, and I'll spring for the room at the *W* to get your freak on,"

Jevon said, thinking of the room he already had, equipped with enough hidden cameras to make a porno movie.

"I'm gon' pass. Besides, you know I'm getting Ariel for the weekend."

"Come on, dog, I can have Cheyenne drop her off to you tomorrow. Shit, tonight is First Friday's Jazz and networking at the *W*. And it's the first hot day of the Spring. And you know ho's be damn near booty-butt-ass naked when it's nice out."

"Did you ever think that Cheyenne might want a night off, being that you're never home?"

"Don't even go there. You know I love my daughter. I just have my needs. Hell, I give her everything as it is."

Everything but your time, Jordan wanted to say.

"Fuck it, you go on and play Super Uncle; I'ma get my groove on. I'll holla." Jevon hung up the cell and merged onto the I-285 ramp.

Chapter 17

*F*orty-five minutes later, Jevon was sitting at a table at the *W* hotel ballroom. He looked down at his mother of pearl Movado watch. It was 6:01. In another hour the fellas would be strolling in.

Jevon got there when he did so that he could catch the early stragglers. He was nursing a glass of Grand Marnier and Coke, watching The Sol Factory on stage, performing a jazz rendition of *People Make The World Go Round* when his hodar (radar for hos) went off.

She looked like she had a basketball under her AKA green skintight skirt. Her back was out, exposing her dark coffee brown skin. She had long, smooth track runner legs, accentuated by matching green stilettos that brought out the definition in her muscular calves.

He stood up and was about to do his thing when he remembered the ring. Like a magician, he quickly made his wedding band disappear into his pants pocket. In the blink of an eye, his brother's missing NFC Championship ring took the wedding band's place.

She stood wide-legged, with her back to the bar. Jevon popped a cinnamon Altoid and made his way over.

As her perfectly round ass came into clearer focus, he mouthed the words, "Wow, wow, wow," when he noticed a crease between her cheeks. "No panties. Thank you, Jesus," he mouthed.

"Excuse me." He lightly touched her arm.

She turned around. "Yes?"

His eyes unconsciously dilated. He searched his mind for a word to describe her face. Ugly wasn't quite it. He was looking at the snake-like scar that ran from her left eye down to the right side of her top lip. And the braids. Her shoulder-length African gold braids and long green fingernails all screamed ghetto fabulous, brainless and most important of all, easy new pussy.

"Hi gorgeous, my name is Jamal." He stuck out his hand, making sure she saw the diamond and gold championship ring. "Can I buy you a drink?" he asked, while holding onto her hand.

She sucked her teeth. "Your name ain't no damn Jamal."

A quizzical look shrouded his face.

"Oh, so you don't remember me, huh?" she asked, her hand still in his.

I have never seen this ho' in my life. I'd remember a scarred-up mothafucka like this. Jordan, she must've thought I was my brother. That's it.

Before he went to prison, Jordan always called his ho's "sweetness." He opened his arms. "Sweetness," he said with a crooked smile on his face. "Where you been?" He sensed the tension between the two easing. "Come on now, give big daddy a hug." He hugged her, pressing his dick against her soft hourglass body.

She pulled away from their embrace. "Why, Jordan? Just please, give me one good reason. Just one."

"Why what?"

Smile, Cherry, smile, she said to herself. *Cheyenne always told her to smile when she felt herself getting angry, and if that didn't work, count backward from ten, she'd said.* "Why'd you leave me in that hotel room? Why didn't you stop—"

"Sweetness, that was then, let's live in the now. Back then, I don't know if you knew, but I was getting high—"

"You actin' real funny, Jordan," she said, with a sideways look on her face. "You know damn well I knew you smoked rock. Hell, how many times did I cop for yo strung-out ass?"

"Look, I'm sorry, but that was years ago, and I've pretty much blocked that part of my life out. I've been clean for five, six years. Right now, I'm just doing me, you know, trynna' live and let live."

"Live and let live," she repeated. "I can't tell. Pssst. The way you left me in that room, never coming to see about—" she closed her eyes and began to count backward.

What the fuck was this bitch talkin' about? Was she about to freak out on me, he wondered as he looked at her closed-eyed stance.

Suddenly she opened her eyes and smiled. She put her hand on the side of his face. "You right, baby. The important thing is what we do now and where we go from here."

"Thanks for understanding." He shook his head. "So much has happened since I last saw you. You just don't know the hell I been through."

The slim, dreaded bartender leaned over the counter.

"I'll have another shot of Grand Marnier." Jevon looked at Cherry. "And the lady will have..." He pointed.

She stuck her tongue out and ran her index finger down the middle of it. "Is that the same finger you used to use," she licked her red lipstick lips, "to play with my pussy?"

Chapter 18

*T*he premature, graying dread-headed bartender
stumbled over his own two feet, nearly dropping a
bottle of Grey Goose on the floor, while Jevon just stood
there staring at Cherry with his mouth hanging open.

She turned to the fumbling young bartender. "Jack and
Coke, light ice, and a shot of tequila with two cherries,
please." She smiled.

"You ain't shy worth a shit, babygirl," Jevon said.

"Shy don't get you nothing but a wet pussy and
cramped fingers."

My type of ho'. He smiled. "Whachu say your name
was again, sweetness?"

*Asshole Joe really didn't remember me. I wonder how
many women he fucked over. How many women he lied to.
How many women he promised the world to. How many
women he played.* "Luscious." She lied. "But everyone
calls me Cherry."

"So how'd you get that name?"

"My ass."

"Your who?"

She turned. "My ass," she said, slapping her palm on the back of her light green skirt. "People used to say that when I walked, my ass was shaped like two huge cherries fucking. What do you think, Jordan?" She rubbed a hand across her ass. "You think my ass looks like two cherries fucking?"

"Sweetness, if two cherries could get their groove on, I would imagine that," he looked at her ass and nodded his approval, "they would look like just like that."

"So, since I like cherries, I began calling myself," she took the cherry out of her drink and stabbed it back and forth with her tongue a few times, "Cherry," she said. "After all, I can't go round telling folks my name is Luscious, they might think I'm a ho'."

Someone needed to tell her that it wasn't the name that suggested that she was a ho'. "I love it," he said, crossing his legs on the barstool and placing his ring hand on his knee.

I bet some airheads were awed by shit like that. She stared at the shiny ring. *I bet he was thinking I was some alley rat, straight out of the projects. Or maybe a dope girl. Some dope boy's play toy.* "I ain't really feeling this place. I ain't into music without no singin'."

"Babygirl," he got up and swayed to the music, "This is Walter Beasley's *Ready for love.* Listen to that piano," he mimicked playing a piano with his fingers on her thighs. "And that horn. Shit, that's real music."

"Nah, real music is what we can be making right now," she grabbed his hand from her thigh, opened her legs and put the hand up her dress. "You feel this wet pussy?"

For the second time tonight, he was speechless, but only for a second. He jerked his hand away before quickly scanning the area to see if anyone was watching. The ballroom was starting to fill up, but no one seemed to be paying any attention to them.

"Ahhh, don't be scared, now," she said.

He turned back to her. "Trust, babygirl, I'm far from scared. I'm just not used to such uhm..."

"A real woman going after what she wants?"

"Yeah. I don't even know where you from, what you do."

She re-crossed her legs and smiled. Toying with him, she said, "Where I'm from makes no difference; it's where I'm at and even more important, where I'll be in an hour or less. But, I'll tell you this, I'm still slaving away at the Super 8 Motel up the street, until I get my demo out," she lied.

"You sing?" he said, more as a question than a statement.

"You don't remember? Ohhhh, that's right," she patted the back of his hand, "you been through a lot." She nodded.

Smart-aleck-ass trick. She think Jordan dogged her ass out. I had a mind to half fuck the whore, get a quick nut, get some head, nut in her mouth, and kick the scarred-up, braid-wearing jungle bitch to the curb. The only reason I wasn't knee-deep up in that pussy right now, is 'cause since Jordan flaked out on me, I needed her dumb ass to help me get Monica's fine ass on video.

"Nah, I rap and write poetry. I'm also writing a book of poems," she said.

"That's cool. I do a little Spoken Word myself," Jevon lied. "You'll have to recite some of your work to me sometime."

They'd had a couple drinks, and she sensed he was getting a little buzzed. "So whachu' do for a livin', pretty eyes? Still getting high?" she asked.

Yeah, high on the thought of my dick being deep up in that ass. "I see you got jokes. A fake smile creased his lips. It's all good, though. I love a woman with a sense of humor." He almost told her that he was into real estate. He nearly forgot that he was Jordan and the woman in front of him was from his brother's other life. No telling what Jordan had told her way back, when he was breaking her off. Jevon wondered why he was trippin'? It was obvious that Jordan didn't tell her he had a twin, but just in case... "I'm working in player relations for the NFL and I'm a socio-activist in the community."

"That's nice."

"So, are you open-minded, Ms. Cherry?"

"Very."

"Oh, really?"

She diverted her attention to the stage. "What's that song the band is playing?" She pointed.

"You like it?"

"Yeah," she got off the bar chair and started swaying to the music, "now that's my shit."

"That's Morris Day and the Time's old school jam *'Gigolo's Get Lonely Too'*."

"Do they now?" she asked.

"Do they what?"

"Do gigolos get lonely, too?"

He shrugged his shoulders. "I wouldn't know."

"Save that for some otha' dumb chick; I know a playa' when I see one."

"Nah, baby, you got..."

"Ah-ah-ah-ah." She waved one of her green glitter fingernails in his direction. "You came up to me because you saw my ass. And from the beginning, your intention was, and is to be," she pointed to her crotch, "up in this. Go 'head, lie. Tell me I'm wrong."

You hit it right on the head, bitch. What did she expect me to say? Whatever I said will mean the difference of me getting to home plate, or striking out. This bitch could very well be the key to me finally fucking that fine-ass Monica. "Whatever I say can, and will, probably be used against me, so," he smiled, "I'm gon' have ta plead the fifth, at least for the moment, but I will answer your question before we part company. Is that fair?"

"Whateva'." She rolled her neck. "I already know the answer. I was just seeing how real you was gon' keep it."

"Alright, babygirl, you wanna keep it real? Let's keep it real."

She smiled and put her hand lightly on his. "Pretty eyes, I don't think you know how to keep anything real?"

Ignoring her snide, he continued. "Can I ask you a question?"

"You *been* askin' me questions."

He leaned in so close that he could feel her breath on his lips. "What's the most spontaneous thing you've ever done?"

Real calm and nonchalant, she said, "Met a chick and her dude at a Publix grocery store and fucked them both in the men's restroom."

"You win," he said, throwing up his hands. "I need you in my life, right now, tonight. What's up?"

"Where?"

"Wherever. My place, here. Matter of fact, why don't we have a threesome?"

"Where is she?"

"I don't know." He reached in his pocket and pulled out his cell phone. "I can damn sure call her though."

"Hope she's a cutie, cause I don't mess with no monkey lookin' females."

"You ever watch that show *Girlfriends*?"

"Every black woman in America has seen that show at one time or another."

"She looks like the broad married to the white guy."

"Ooooooooookay, why you ain't got her on the phone, already?"

Chapter 19

" *M*y stuff is on fire, girl. I can't even look at a banana without squeezing my legs together," Monica said.

"Don't feel like the Lone Ranger, girl, I'm in the same boat."

"Cheyenne, you ain't even in the same body of water my boat's in. You go to bed with that fine-ass Jevon Hayes, every night. You aren't getting' none cause you don't want none."

The church switchboard lit up.

"Hold on, girl, one of my lines is ringing," Monica said.

On a Friday afternoon? Cheyenne said to herself.

"Beautiful Baptist, Monica Wiley speaking." She spoke in her sweetest First Lady voice. "No, ma'am, the church picnic is next Saturday, April 10th... No ma'am it's not tomorrow...Okay, thank you and you have a blessed day." After putting the headset back on the receptionist's desk, she picked the cell phone back up. "Girl, your people are straight ignorant. For the last month, banners and flyers were all over the church, announcing the day and time of the annual church picnic."

"Sounds like a lot of someones need to get hooked on phonics," Cheyenne said.

"Nah, they need to stop following my blind-ass, horny, black leprechaun husband."

"Blind leadin' the blind," Cheyenne said.

"You ain't never lied, girl. And how 'bout, just in the last couple hours, I've had at least twenty calls and three members come by with bags of chips and plastic utensils, thinking the picnic is tomorrow."

"Why they bringin' food? I thought the twenty dollars a head covered food and activities."

"It does. You know how *your* people is," Monica said.

"They aren't *my* people. I quit claiming them after the NAACP endorsed Hillary," Cheyenne said.

"I know, girl. They should change the name to the NAAWW, the National Association for the Advancement of White Women. And don't forget about Tavis."

Cheyenne chimed back in. "Girl, please don't get me started on him. As intelligent and well-spoken as he is, you'd think he'd understand that Barack couldn't have won running on a racial platform. We make up thirteen percent of the population, and take away the felons that can't vote, the children, and the totally unconnected, and we might get two percent of blacks to the polls."

"Your people," Monica said.

"You know I got Seminole blood in me. I'm officially throwing my black card in the trash and claiming only the Native American side of my family," Cheyenne said.

"If you can do that, knowing damn well your black-ass a direct descendant of Kunta Kinte, then I'm Hispanic."

"Monica, you about as Hispanic as a Taco Bell in the Mississippi bayou."

They both laughed.

"Girl, what are you doing at church on a Friday evening, anyway?" Cheyenne asked her best friend.

"Same thing you doin' at home on a Friday evening." She sighed. "Being bored out of my mind, playing keep-away from CW."

"You say you horny; I don't see why you just don't give the man some."

"Some what? Girl, The way he goin' around screwin' strippers. I'll be damned if he give me something. Shit, I'm just waitin' for his little ding-a-ling to fall off."

"Monica, you crazy."

"Nah, you crazy. If I was married to a six-foot-something, bronzed, hazel-eyed, big-hand, big-foot, swollen-lipped man like you got, it would always be off and popping up in that big-ass house of yours."

"I guess you through with women, too?" Cheyenne said.

"Women are cool, but a tongue and a strap-on just cannot replace a sweat-glistening, live, shit-talkin', tall, dark, strong, handsome, big-dick black man like you got. My panties are getting' wet just thinking about your husband's twin, dick deep up in me."

"Okay, I know we close, girl, but that's a little too much information," Cheyenne said. "And you know Jordan's off limits."

"I know, I know, but a girl can dream, right? Besides, it's just a matter of time before that Jerry Springer shit you got goin' on over there come to a head."

"I know," she said.

"You still gon' tell Jordan how you feel when he comes to pick up Ariel this evening?"

"I don't know."

"Girl, if you don't quit trippin' and tell him everything."

"I don't know. He won't even look me in the eye. His conversation always sounds scripted. I think he despises me for marrying Jevon."

"If he does, it's because he don't know who his brother really is," Monica said.

"Who am I to shatter his image of Jevon?"

"A woman who is so in love with her husband's twin that she'd rather masturbate and be miserable than give her fine-ass husband any."

"On that note, let me go. I have to shower and change."

"For what?" I thought you were in for the night."

"I am, but Jordan will be here any minute to pick up Ariel. I just want to look presentable," Cheyenne said.

"If Ariel weren't there, I'd think you were trying to cool your hot-ass faucet off."

"Bye, girl," Cheyenne said, before hanging up.

Monica sat back in the brown leather swivel chair behind the large round desk in the receptionist area of the church administration building, arms behind her head. She knew Jevon wasn't shit, but yet and still, he'd been giving her stronger fuck-me signs for months now. She had to admit, she was throwing signs right back at him. Whenever they were in the same room, he'd lick his lips right as she glanced his way. And she would find a reason to walk past him rubbing her hips or ass up against him.

If he only knew what she wanted to do to him. If she got with any man in or outside of the church, she figured

Wild Cherry

Jevon was her safest bet. She would've gotten with Jordan, but he acted like he didn't like pussy anymore.

Just this morning, Monica awoke on the verge of having an earthquake orgasm. She'd been dreaming of Jevon. It was the same dream she'd had for the past three nights.

*****

They were naked. It was night outside, pitch dark. Each warm raindrop sent erotic chills through her body. The alley they stood in lit up every so often as streaks of lightning electrified the midnight sky. She knew they were near a busy street because, between hair-raising bursts of thunder, she heard the humming of cars speeding by, splashing puddles of water on some sidewalk nearby.

Jevon was standing straight up, like some naked black Roman warrior about to go into battle. He held his long, C-shaped, tree trunk, pulsating dick in his hand like a weapon.

She looked at his huge feet. The curly hair on his legs. His muscled thighs. The round pinkish head of his manhood. The waves in his stomach that raindrops seemed to swim down. The little crayon-brown nipples on his chest. His thick, strong neck. His chiseled facial features. Those puffy, lickable lips, and then the eyes. Those strong, hazel brown, hypnotizing eyes. Before she knew it, her legs were wrapped around his back. Her arms were draped around his neck like fine jewelry. Not a word passed between them.

Hungrily, he passionately licked her teeth, her tongue, sucked her lips, and worked his way to the back of her ear, her secret spot.

"Oooh," she moaned.

103

Her back was against a brick wall. The warm rain started to pour extremely hard, intensifying their hunger for each other.

His strong hands palmed her ass cheeks like a basketball. He went down on one knee, holding her in the air, like a gift to the heavens. He worked his long, thick, wet tongue, like a young Ali in a title fight, jab, jab, uppercut, over tongue, right. It felt like multiple tongues were everywhere around and inside her soaking-wet womanhood.

"Oh got-damn," she said aloud, squirming in the leather chair, not realizing she was daydreaming.

She felt her body convulsing. "I'm cumming," she shouted.

In one swift motion, Jevon stood and turned her around, so that her hands were on the wall. She now stood straight legged, with her back slightly bent over, her hands touching the rough exterior red brick wall. Hard rain drops, pounded her back, and swam down her butt, between her cheeks and dripped from her wet pink clit, further electrifying her sexual sensation. Her pussy was screaming for a taste of his manhood.

"Please, I need to feel you. Fuck me. Fuck me got dammit!" she demanded.

A burst of thunder exploded and lightening lit up the black night, as he drove all nine inches of diamond hard dick in her.

"Fuck!" she said between gasps.

Chapter 20

*M*onica's eyes popped open as her cell phone vibrated between her legs.

She wiped her hand, and the wet cell phone on the ruffles of her tennis skirt.

"Hello?"

"May I speak with Monica?"

"This is she."

"Are you alone?" the soft female voice asked.

"Who is this?"

"You don't know me, but I am five-six, my skin is the color of midnight and it's soft and baby-ass smooth. I'm a size six, I'm in very good shape and, best of all, my waxed pussy stays as wet as my mouth."

Unconsciously, Monica closed her eyes, licked her index and forefinger and placed them back under her skirt.

"I'm in the grand ballroom of the *W* hotel having drinks with this sexy man who goes by the name of Jordan, and he has me soaking wet telling me about a fantasy of having his monster dick in you while my tongue is playing with the ball on and around your clit."

*No way. I tried to give him some pussy the day he got
out of prison. Nigga ain't had no pussy in five years and he
turned me down. We ain't had two words since I cursed his
ass out and called him a faggot in front of everyone at his
coming-home party.*

"Are you still there?" the woman speaking to Monica
asked.

"Yes," she paused, "I'm-I'm here."

"Well, that is a problem, now isn't it?"

"Excuse me?" Monica said.

"You're there and Jordan's dick and my magical tongue
are at the *W* hotel. But, I think we are on our way over to
Jordan's house. Now, if you can come, we all can cum over
and over and over."

"Give me an hour. I'll be there," Monica said.

"You need the address?"

"No, I know where he lives, right over by the AU
center campus, right?"

"Jordan, here," she heard the woman say, "She thinks
you live in the West End. Give her your address."

"Hey, babygirl," Jevon said. "You got somethin' to
write with?"

"Okay, I'm ready."

"Where you coming from?" he asked.

"Just give me the address; I'll put it in the 745's
navigation system."

"Just come to the *W* hotel, downtown. I'm gon' get a
room. Call me when you're pulling up," he said.

"Jordan? Why you sound funny?" Monica asked.

"I'm back." The female voice was back on the cell.
"What? You wanna speak back to him?"

Monica looked down at the caller I.D. and smiled. "No,
no. I'll see you two in a few."

Chapter 21

$\mathcal{T}$he hotel's signature maroon comforter slid to the floor as he pounded Monica from behind.

"Unh-uh, harder, harder baby. Ooooooo-ooo-ooo, yeah, like that, baby, right there. You hittin' my spot, got-damn. Ooooh shit. Fuck this pussy."

"Who's your daddy?" he asked, slowly removing and re-inserting all eight plus inches of his pole-hard manhood in and out of her hungry wet love canal.

"O-O, Oh you-you are. Slap my ass harder, baby," Monica shouted.

"Who's pussy is this?"

Scrunch, scrit, scrot. Her wet pussy was making noises as if it were answering his question.

"Yours, daddy, oh my, damn. Fuck me, daddy. I'm about to cum."

Jevon was sitting on his legs, his back was flat on the bed, and his biceps were bulging. Sweat was rolling down the ripples of his stomach muscles as he curled and lifted his wife's best friend up and down off of his bone-hard member.

Five years of doing yoga made it so he could comfortably fuck and cum in positions that most women couldn't even imagine.

"Does the good Bishop fuck you like this?" he asked while changing gears and speeding up."

"Oh-oh, I'm-I'm cummin', I'm cummin' again." Her back muscles tensed, her legs started shaking. "Cum with me, boo."

He wanted to wipe the sweat from his eyes, but Monica had said those magic words, *I'm cumming.* He couldn't see, so he blinked several times, trying to get the sweat in his eyes to dissolve. He was so tired. He felt like his heart was about to explode. He felt a Charlie horse beginning in his left foot, but still, he couldn't stop. Not yet. Jevon was thirty-three, and in all his years he'd never excelled at any physical activity except sex. He secretly wished that someone would come up with a Sex Olympics, so he could get recognition at being the best at something.

"Oh-oh-oh, here it is, daddy. Don't move. Right there. Shitttttttt!"

He felt her pussy contracting.

She lurched forward trying to get away. His dick almost came out. "Oh, hell no you don't," he said, catching his fourth wind. "You ain't getting away from this dick yet. No, not 'til I bust," he said while wrapping his arms around her waist and pumping, jackhammer fast.

Five minutes later, he no longer felt his legs or feet. Sweat flew everywhere as he hit every wall of her insides.

"You feel that? Huh?" He gritted his teeth, while exploding inside her.

"OOOOOO, I'm cumin,' too. Oh-oh, oh-o-o-o-o," Cherry announced.

So caught up in the moment, Jevon almost forgot Cherry was in the same bed.

The whole time, Cherry was on her knees sucking Monica's nipples while playing with the Bullet that vibrated on her own clit.

The Bullet was one of many vibrators Jevon had kept in what he called his goodie bag. He often joked about it being like an American Express card. He never left home without it because he never knew when he was going to get lucky.

The inventor of Viagra should get the Nobel Peace Prize, he thought. All he took was half a pill and it seemed that his dick stayed hard forever.

After he came, he pushed Monica off of him and rolled to a dry spot at the foot of the bed to catch his breath and massage his legs and cramped feet. His eyes began to dilate as he watched one of Monica's long red fingernails slowly travel from Cherry's neck and down her spine.

"Uhmmm, ohhh," Cherry moaned, as Monica's tongue tickled the back of her earlobe.

Unconsciously, Jevon's hands had gone from rubbing his numb legs and cramped foot to massaging his still hard, at-attention member.

"Damn," he said, as Cherry did a Houdini, making Monica's 36 C cups slowly disappear inside her mouth and reappear a few seconds later. "Uhm, Uhm, Uhm," he said, wondering if she could do that with his dick.

He reached over the side of the bed and lifted the comforter from the floor and wiped his face before sitting up and grabbing Monica by the waist and turning her to face him.

"Woman," he gazed into her eyes, "I've wanted you for so damn long," he said, before gently laying her down and placing her peanut butter-colored legs over his broad shoulders.

"This the way you want it, baby?"

"Nah, is this the way you want it?" he asked while toying with Monica, barely inserting the head of his penis in and out of her gushing wetness.

"Uhmmm, yeah, baby. You got my pussy creamin' and screamin'. You feel how wet I am?"

Suddenly his entire body tightened. He couldn't think, he couldn't speak. "Ha! Ha! Haaa! Ooooh." He sounded like a wounded animal. He'd never felt anything remotely like what he was feeling now. Cherry had several Halls cough drops in her mouth, rolling them around his balls as she gently took them in and out of her mouth, while sticking a finger in his ass.

"I'm cu-cu-ah-ah. Shit!" he screamed as the thick lotion-like juice shot up Monica's chest.

"What the hell?" he asked, pushing Monica's legs off his shoulders and turning toward Cherry.

"You like? Cherry asked, barely touching his nipples, sending even more jolts of erotic electricity through his convulsing body.

He pulled Cherry up by her arms making sure that her mouth couldn't get near his body. It took a minute for him to regain control.

"Damn, won-wonder woman," he looked down to see what type condition his dick was in. For the briefest of moments he contemplated getting up and getting a condom from his goodie bag, but Cherry's erotic moaning killed that thought. "I'm about to fuck you into next week," he said, pushing Cherry off the bed and onto the gray carpeted floor.

"Don't sing it. Bring it, nigga," she said, standing up and bending over, bracing her hands on the edge of the hotel's king-size bed.

He no longer had any feeling in his dick, or much anywhere else. Common sense should have told him to rest a bit, get a condom, but common sense didn't make him cum like the scar-faced woman with the slick mouth.

He stood behind her admiring her track-star tight body.

Cherry turned her head. "Nigga, you need a written invitation."

"It's smart ass bitches like you that make a nigga pull out a red cape and a big-ass S."

"Supermouth, if you don't shut the hell up and gimme that—"

"Guh," she gulped as he grabbed her waist and rammed himself inside her love tunnel.

Like an oil drill, he went in and out. Cherry smelled clean, and with a pretty pussy like hers, she had to be straight, he rationalized. Fuck a condom. And as far as Bishop Poo-nanny's wife was concerned, well, that was another story. There was no tellin' who and what CW was running up in without protection. Oh, hell, too late for regrets now. And, hell, the Viagra wasn't showing any signs of letting up, so why should he?

"Damn, girl, yo' pussy feel like hot butter," he said.

In his stand-up routines back in the 70's, the king of comedy, Richard Pryor used to always talk about that all-allusive snapping pussy. Pussy that'll make you disown your own momma. *Well, I've found it,* Jevon thought, as he explored Cherry's cave. The scar on her face made her as ugly as hell, but that pussy was heaven.

"You, mothafucka," Cherry shouted. "Beat it up, nigga," she said, backing into his powerful thrusts.

He slapped her ass. "This my pussy. I own this shit."

"No, the hell it ain't, nigga. Not half-fucking me like you doin'."

What the fuck? No, she didn't, he thought while wrapping a hand around the back of her neck for traction.

"Squeeze, nigga, my neck won't break."

Tired of that smart-ass mouth, he took his dick out and without any warning, he aimed the torpedo-shaped head of his pole, before he rammed himself into her asshole.

"That's it. Nigga, make it do what it do. Make it do what it mothafuckin' do," she said as he squeezed the back of her neck harder.

He couldn't believe she was still able to talk with his dick in her ass. So, he took a deep breath and wrapped her braids around one hand, while the other had her neck in a death grip. Pulling her hair, and gripping her neck, he started pumping in and out of her like a man possessed.

"Talk that shit now, woman. Huh... I don't hear that mouth now," he said, pumping at record speed. "I'm King Big Dick, Mr. Magic, and you bet' not ever forget that shit."

"Shit, damn, fuck, fuck, fuck, fuck, damn!" The whole seventh floor of the hotel must've heard Cherry as she hollered and shouted a dictionary of obscenities.

Monica watched the scene in awe.

Cherry's eyes bulged. She began to silently gag.

"Jevon, she can't breathe," Monica shouted. You're choking her."

His eyes were squeezed shut. He was a machine. He didn't even hear Monica call him by his name instead of Jordan's. He didn't feel Cherry's body convulse. He opened his eyes. "Ahhhh," he shouted, exploding for the seventh time in a little over three hours.

Wild Cherry

"Jevon," Monica screamed, right before Cherry lost consciousness and collapsed.

Chapter 22

*J*evon hadn't moved. He stood in the same place, breathing hard and staring at Cherry's lifeless body sprawled on the floor at the foot of the king-size hotel bed.

"Oh my God, Oh my God," Monica repeated scrambling off of the bed and to the floor where Cherry's lifeless body laid. "What were you doing?" Monica looked up at Jevon. "What were you thinking? You didn't hear me tell you she couldn't breathe?"

He just stood statue-still, naked as the day he was born, not saying a word.

She felt for a pulse. "What did you do?"

"Is she... Is she..."

Monica looked up. "I think so."

"Noooo! No! No!" He shook his head back and forth. "What are we gon' do?"

Monica went to grabbing her clothes. "*We* didn't fuck her to death. So *we* ain't gon' do shit. Now, *I'm* getting the hell outta here."

"You just gon' leave me here alone with her?"

114

"Damn straight. I'm the First Lady of the third largest church in the southeast. Do you know what kind of scandal there'll be if word gets out that the First Lady had a threesome with her best friend's husband."

"How did you know?"

"Know what?" she asked.

"That I wasn't Jordan."

She held up her cell phone. "Caller I.D.," she said, sitting on the bed putting her other shoe on.

"Damn, I forgot to block my number out," he said.

A few seconds later, she opened the hotel room door with caution and looked outside.

"What am I gon' do?"

She turned back to him. "Pray," she said, before entering the lavish hotel hallway.

Twenty minutes later, Jevon was downstairs sitting on a barstool, washing down four Tylenols with two shots of Absolut Vodka. First Fridays was still going on strong. He looked at his watch; it was only five past one. He racked his mind wondering what to do. A woman was upstairs, dead in *his* hotel room, with *his* DNA all up inside her. The hotel was registered in *his* name. The hotel room had been supplemented with Monica's husband's hidden cameras. The same cameras with *his* fingerprints all over them.

That's it, he thought. He pulled out a twenty and dropped it on the bar before getting up and rushing out.

He stood in the hotel lobby dialing Bishop Wiley's cell.

"Shit! Shit! Shit!" he said each time the man's voicemail picked up.

He set all this shit in motion. *If I hadn't agreed to set his wife up, none of this shit would've happened,* he thought.

Fuck it. Mothafucka don't wanna call me back, I'll just figure a way to get Cherry out of the hotel and into my car, and I'll just drive over to the Wiley estate and drop her dead ass off at the front gate, he said to himself while watching the hotel lobby spin around.

He looked at his watch while stumbling toward the hotel lobby elevator. It read: 2:15. He'd been gone a little over an hour.

As soon as he got off of the elevator, he took his cell phone out and was about to try CW one more time, before it vibrated in his hand.

"CW, we have a pro'lem?"

"It better be a national emergency. Negro, you called my phone seventeen times in thirty minutes."

"Where you be?" Jevon asked.

"Why?"

"I got your girl on candid camera."

"Excuse me?" Bishop Wiley asked.

"Mocina, Moni, Moci, Monica," he said slobbering.

"Babydoll, I'll be back in a minute," Jevon heard CW say before coming back to the phone. "Jevon, tell me you aren't drunk. Tell me—"

"Your wife," he interrupted. "Man, she got some mafinicent, I mean magicent..."

"Magnificent, fool," CW interrupted.

"Yeah, see, we agree. Bish, let me tell ya, she got that bow-wow, top-notch, snapper. Yes, sir. I fucked the dog shit outta her and I got it all on camera."

"You are drunk," CW said.

"I may be a little tat, teenie-weenie tipsy, but I'm telling you some good shit. I did her for you, but that ain't why I'm callin'." The phone got quiet.

Seconds later, CW said, "I'm waiting."

"On what?" Jevon asked.

"Why else are you calling my phone at two in the morning?"

"Where you at?"

"Jevon, I'm hanging up this phone if you don't start making some sense right now."

"I can't actually go into pariculars, particu-details over the phone, but some serious shit done happened and you need to get us outta this shit."

"Us?"

"Yeah, us, me, you, us. U damn S. Now look here. I'm at the uhh, shit, where the hell am I at." He looked around the hotel hallway, until his eyes rested on the large W that was on the elevator doors. "The *W* Hotel, downtown. You can come down here or I can come to you. I swear, man, we have an emergency simulation on our hands."

"I don't see how *we* have an emergency situation on *our* hands," CW corrected, "especially since I'm where I am and you're where you are. I have no doubt that *you* have an emergency situation, but *we* don't have any business other than an exchange of money for *my* cameras. So this *us* and *we* stuff is non-existent."

"Look, you can come down here or there's no telling what I'll say under pressure facing life in the penitentiary."

"Don't threaten me. Don't you ever threaten—"

"I'm not threat—"

"Meet me at Café Intermezzo on Peachtree in thirty minutes," CW said before hanging up.

"Who fuck think he is?" Jevon said, further discombobulating his words. "I'm a grown-ass man." Jevon shadow boxed the air in the elevator hallway. "I'll whip that Barbie doll-size, Katt Williams-perm-wearin', undercover faggot, false-preachin' mufucka's ass," Jevon said aloud while stumbling down the hall toward his room. "Who in hell you two lookin' at, shrimp-fried-rice-eatin' mothafuckas?" He said to a young Asian couple hurrying toward the elevator. "Ack like a nigga ain't s'pposed to be in a nice-ass hotel."

A minute later he fumbled with the hotel key card. Moments later he opened the door and stumbled into the room. "Why the hell don't they put these damn light switches where a nigga can find 'em?" he said running his hands across the wall. "Ha, ha," he said flicking the light switch on. His eyes got big as a moment of clarity hit him like a Brinks truck. "What the?"

Chapter 23

"*H*ell if I'm gon' feel guilty. There's no way in hell I'm gon' risk everything I've worked for these past three years to help another dirty-dick nigga. The dick was good, damn good, but God ain't made a dick good enough to make me lose my damn mind," Monica mumbled. She was lying in bed, staring at the bright screen on her cell phone.

Jevon wasn't shit his damn self, playing everyone around him. Serves him right, she thought. Monica had been wrestling with her guilt over leaving the scene of a crime. No, she reasoned. She wasn't a doctor. She didn't know for sure if the woman was dead, and if she was, she didn't do it.

She looked at the phone, willing herself not to call. Knowing Jevon's scary ass, he probably figured out a way to get rid of the body.

She shook her head. She wouldn't go back. She was going to pretend this day had never happened. If she did go back, three years of planning and eighteen years of praying for the opportunity to kill her husband, Bishop C. Wendell Wiley would be for naught.

*****

Three years ago, Monica met the then Reverend C. Wendell Wiley at a private wake for his wife, who'd fought, and lost a long battle with breast cancer. It had cost Monica a couple hundred dollars and a small piece of her pride, when she let the security gate guard put his hands up her dress. All this to get through the massive wrought-iron security gates guarding the entrance to the two-million-dollar Wiley Mexican villa, located in the Atlanta suburb of Alpharetta.

Monica wore a short, but tasteful form-fitting black dress. Her long Hawaiian silky black weave was pulled back into a ponytail. The three-inch open-toe heels she wore increased her height to nearly six-feet, mostly legs, which were on full display as two ushers led her down a long hall and into the peach and cream marbled floored gymnasium sized den area.

Monica remembered being in complete awe as she had surveyed the eclectic art studio like walls. She remembered thinking that that one room was larger than the three-bedroom project-housing apartment she'd lived in with her foster sister, Joanne and her five kids.

She'd walked around the room patiently waiting, stalking her prey. At that time it had been fifteen years. Fifteen years since C. Wendell Wiley had molested her when she was twelve. It was the most painful, terrifying, experience she'd ever had. And the beating she took after confiding in her foster mother hurt almost as worse as him forcing himself inside her, tearing at the insides of her young pre-adolescent body. After Ms. Linda, her fourth foster mother savagely beat and called her a liar and a whore for accusing Reverend Wiley of such a thing, she never told anyone about that horrific day, no one except for Cheyenne. For years she had horrible nightmares and panic attacks when left in dark rooms. What kept her out of a mental hospital were her daydreams. Dreams of revenge. She often sat in school, at work, and up in bed dreaming of ways to expose, humiliate, and finally kill the man that stole her innocence.

She walked up to him, gently took his hand, and slowly enunciated her words so he could see every muscle in her thick lips contract. She'd said, "Reverend Wiley, I'm so, so very sorry. I know what it's like to lose someone."

"Thank you, and you are?" he asked, holding a half-filled goblet with some sort of brown liquid swirling around inside.

His breath almost made her stomach turn. His facial expression showed no signs of recognition. Speak slow and fluid, girl. Proper and prim, just like Cheyenne. No slang. Proper and prim, she had said to herself. "My name is Monica." Her dark brown eyes flirted with his. "Monica Sommers."

They stood in one of four rear corners on the opposite side of the room where his wife's body rested in a capsule-like stainless-steel casket.

"Forgive me, but I don't recall ever," he'd looked her up and down, "seeing you at Beautiful Baptist."

What had he been eating, wolf ass? "Really?" she'd said.

He nodded.

"I've seen and heard some of your fiery sermons."

"So, you're not a member?" he'd asked.

"No, not yet," she'd said, still holding his well-manicured hand.

"How'd you get in here?" he'd asked.

Avoiding his breath, and breathing fresh air, she had turned her head, looking toward the crowd, standing around his wife's casket. "I just had to say my goodbyes to Ms. Pam."

"You knew my wife?"

"Well, sort of." She turned back around. He didn't even attempt to divert his eyes from her bulging breasts. "I met her at Grady hospital a while back. My aunt was in her last stages of lung cancer, and your wife sat with her and I before she died. It meant a lot to me, especially since she, too, had cancer."

He placed the goblet on the table next to where they stood, and placed a hand on her shoulder. "However you got in, I don't care." He smiled, exposing a flawless set of capped teeth. "I'm just glad you're here."

She sucked in her bottom lip. "I am, too." She squeezed his hand. "If there is anything Reverend Wiley, and I mean anything, I can do to make you feel better, please don't hesitate to call," she said, mysteriously producing a colorful business card.

"A dance instructor?"

She began to feel sick as memories of that dreadful night when she was twelve dredged up in her mind.

"What type of dance do you instruct?"

The hand. The hand she held was one of the two that had wedged her legs apart all those years ago. Possibly the same hand that had covered her mouth, while he'd ravaged her young body. Tears began to well up in her eyes. She had started to feel as if the room was closing in on her. She had wanted to let go of his hand but she couldn't.

"Are you okay?" he had asked.

"Yes, I'm just having a moment. Your wife," she said, feigning grief.

He had broken the spell, removing his hand from hers to reach into his pocket and hand her some tissue.

"Thank you," she said taking the tissue and silently counting backward from ten and remembering something else Cheyenne had taught her. When you come face to face with the Reverend, if you get nervous, just imagine him naked with a diaper on, Cheyenne had said.

He went on. "I was asking what type of dance you taught. I may want to learn myself," he'd said with a sly grin on his face.

"Pole," she had said, regaining her composure.

"Say, say again?"

"You know pole dancing, strip tease," she'd said.

"Oh, really now?"

She smiled, almost ready to burst out in laughter as she'd pictured Reverend Wiley wearing a Victoria Secrets two piece, red lace bra and panties. "Yes, really now," she'd said, back in full control.

"Babydoll," he smiled, "can you make that booty bounce like they do in rap videos."

"I can make it bounce, and rock and roll like you can't even begin to imagine, sweetheart." She looked at all five-foot-six of him, as he stood at an angle wearing a black tailored suit.

"Where do I sign up?" he asked.

"You wanna learn how to work a pole?" she asked.

"No. Unh-uh." He shook his head. "I work my pole just fine. I wanna watch you work a pole."

"I just bet you do. And I take it you have a special pole in mind?"

"Reverend, there you are. Oh my Lord, God, Jesus, Mary, Joseph, and Paul, I am so sorry." An older woman had stepped between them.

Monica pointed to the business card she'd handed the Reverend before mouthing the words, "Call me" before she had walked away.

Early the next day, he'd called, wanting to get together later that evening after the funeral.

Monica didn't let him take her out until a couple nights after the funeral. That was also the same night she put Annie poo-nanny on him. She took him to heaven and fucked the hell out of him all at the same time. At one point she'd made his dick disappear inside her mouth. During this time, her index finger made figure eights on his dark brown nipples while the index finger from her other hand was playing with his balls. The way he went to screamin', she had thought he was gon' keel over and have a heart attack in his own California king-size bed. He'd called on Jesus, Moses, God, and some others before his eyes rolled into the back of his head.

Before she had gone home at three in the morning she had the reverend sprung and speaking in tongue.

For six months, she had sparingly rationed out her sex. She had to bide his and her time. Whenever she had given him a taste, he lost his mind.

After the third month she had surprised him and brought another woman into the bedroom. Instead of joining, he'd just stood over his bed with a jar of Murray's grease, jerking himself off while the two women went at it.

Many times he'd attempted to shower her with money and gifts, but each time she declined his generosity. Him in a casket was the only gift she wanted. But even that wasn't good enough. He had to suffer. He had to be humiliated. He had to lose everything he'd built and was building.

She rationalized that if she'd accepted the diamond tennis bracelets or the car he offered to buy, then he'd have control. This was her game. And it would be played by her rules.

At the four-month mark of their relationship he had started using the 'L' word. Due to her recent money shortage, she decided to move into a penthouse apartment CW owned. She really didn't want to, but she was tired of him pressuring her about where she had lived and worked.

Not long after he'd begun using the L word, she trapped him. The entire time they'd been together she'd been taking estrogen and she had had a specialist administer fertility shots. But none of that would've helped without his seed. She'd tried to convince him that he didn't need to use a condom. And each time he had ignored her. She told him she was on birth control, but that didn't matter. He'd said his seed was sacred, that it would only be shared with his wife.

So, after moving into his penthouse, he'd let his guard down, letting her remove and dispense of the condoms after they had sex. And each time, she'd gone into the restroom, removed the syringe-like turkey baster she had hidden, and extracted his seed and shot it into her.

A couple months later, she had stood over the bed in his apartment and said, "I'm pregnant."

He'd shaken the cob webs from his head. "Say again?"

"I'm pregnant, with your child."

"My child." He'd patted a hand on his bare chest, before bursting out in laughter.

"What's so damn funny?" she'd asked.

"What you just said."

From early on as a child she couldn't stand anyone laughing at her.

Control, girl. Control. Don't let him see who you are. You've worked too hard and too long to go instant mothafucka on him. Keep the hood in you, like you have for eight months. "And what does that mean?" she'd asked.

He'd pulled the satin sheets back and swung a leg over the side of the bed.

Amazing how one word, specifically the big P word could make a player's steel hard-on turn into soft putty, she'd thought.

He smiled. "Sister Monica, if you're pregnant—"

"If?"

"Yes, if. And if you say you are, I believe you, but me being the father is impossible. Number one," he counted on his fingers, "I always use protection. Two, I have a low sperm count, and three if there is a baby inside you and you haven't been with anyone else you better get used to being called Mary, and you better start calling me Joseph."

She had crossed her arms. "One," she counted on her fingers, "you are the only man I've slept with since I met you. Two, you have a low sperm count, not a no sperm count. And three, seventy percent of condoms have microscopic holes in them, and four, I will not name our son Jesus, because there is nothing miraculous about this baby I'm carrying, Daddy."

A month later the DNA test had come back conclusive. She had laughed in his face, turning down the fifty grand he'd offered her to have an abortion. Eventually he realized the only way to get rid of her was to kill her. And that he tried on more than one occasion.

A month after a man was arrested for trying to run her over as she walked to her car with a bag full of groceries in her arms, she became Mrs. Monica Wiley. Five months after they were married, she slipped on some grease and fell down the stairs at the Wiley Estate. The Reverend was never charged or even questioned in either incident. Although she didn't lose the baby either time, the trauma from the fall on the stairs caused her child to be stillborn.

Chapter 23

*a*fter years of living in hell planning the devil's demise, it was way past time for Bishop Wiley to be exposed, humiliated, and then killed by her hands, and she'd die making sure that every step of her plan succeeded. No, she would not go back to the hotel. No, she would not help Jevon.

Monica heard the alarm chirp, indicating that CW was creeping in. She looked at the clock on her phone. It was nearly four in the morning.

"Unhh," she grunted, hating the man she was married to.

Jevon was weak. Who was she kidding? If he did get the body out of the hotel, what would he do with it? He'd get caught, and then he'd be charged with murder or some other felony, and just like he'd lied and had his own brother locked up, he would surely lie on her, too. And, the entire situation would end her reign as First Lady. She couldn't stand to think of the sympathy CW would receive from the congregation.

Wild Cherry

She placed her phone on a goose down pillow before slipping out of bed. She knelt down and reached under the bed, retrieving the red-handled axe she kept in case of an emergency. Next, she walked into the bathroom, closed the door, and waited.

It was over, she had to do it. It was only a matter of time before they caught up with Jevon, if they hadn't already. If she was going to prison it would be for homicide, not for fleeing the scene of a homicide. It felt like an elephant was removed from her shoulders as a surreal calm came over her. She closed her eyes as she raised the axe, upon hearing CW enter the bedroom's French double doors. A tear of joy, relief, and finality streaked down her face as she stood behind the door waiting. Waiting for her victim. She was tired, but yet energized. She'd waited so long for this moment. She just prayed for God to send her to the same hell He sent the bishop to, so she could spend eternity killing him over and over.

He was so close she could hear his breathing. A maniacal smile covered her face and she squeezed the wooden axe handle, poised to swing as he turned the bathroom doorknob.

Chapter 24

"*G*od damn you to hell," she screamed.

He fell to the ground screaming, "Noooo!"

The axe handle struck his back, the blade barely missing his flesh.

"Jevon?" Monica shouted, letting go of the wooden handle.

Shivering and rolled up into a ball, in a high-pitched voice sober as a surgeon, Jevon shouted, "Woman, are you crazy?"

Monica was on her knees beside him, in front of the bathroom door. "Oh, Jevon, I'm so, so sorry. Are you hurt?"

"I don't know. I... What the—"

"I thought... I thought you was C, a burglar. I mean, I thought you were a burglar."

He turned and lay on his back.

She used her index finger to wipe a tear from his face. "You wanna tell me what you doin' in here, Jevon?"

"The door was unlocked."

"I didn't ask you how you got in."

"I climbed the fence."

"Jevon!"

"Okay, okay," he said sitting up. "Ouch!" He arched his back. "You almost broke my back with that axe handle. Damn, that shit hurt," he said, rubbing his back.

"Not as bad as it will if you don't tell me what you're doing inside my house at four-something in the morning."

"Cherry. She's gone."

"I know that, fool, I was there—"

"No, no, no." He shook his head. "She's literally gone," Jevon said, admiring Monica in her peach teddy, one that left very little to the imagination.

"Get your mind out the gutter and finish," she said.

"My mind is far from being in a gutter."

"You know what I mean, Jevon."

"Okay, okay. After you left, I went back to the ballroom and had a drink, trying to sort shit out in my mind. I was gone maybe forty-five minutes, an hour tops. So, anyway, I goes back to the room and she was gone. Her clothes, everything."

"Fool, that means, she wasn't dead," Monica said as a wave of relief and calm blew through her mind.

"But, you felt for a pulse."

Now, I can take my time and re-think how I'm going to kill him, without going to prison.

"Monica?"

She looked into Jevon's eyes. "I'm sorry. What did you say?"

"I said, you told me that Cherry was dead."

"No, I said that I couldn't *feel* a pulse."

"If she didn't have a pulse, then that meant-"

She interrupted. "And when did I graduate from med—
"

His pinkish-brown lips on hers prevented Monica from finishing. The kiss was long and passionate. She gasped. "Jevon."

"Monica," he replied, lifting the teddy over her head.

"Too many buttons," she said, beginning to unbutton his shirt. "Fuck this. Uhmm," she said ripping his shirt open, exposing his smooth, muscular chest.

He turned her over. She, on her knees and he, in back of her. "Where's the bishop?" he managed to ask while rubbing the head of his penis up, down, and around her wetness.

"Oooooooooh, yeah," she cooed while using a finger to play with her clit. "In hell, I hope," she said, anxiously waiting to feel his torpedo inside her. Her head was nearly under the bed, but she could care less. "Fuck me, Jevon. Fuck me right now, baby," she begged, her butt in the air and her hard nipples pressed against the bamboo hardwood bedroom floor.

"This ain't right. Ohh, shit, this ain't even right," he said, inserting the head of his steel-hard manhood. "Damn, you are so, so wet."

"You make me wet, baby."

"I swear this ain't right, Monica. What if he walks in?"

"Fuck him."

Chapter 25

"**F**uck me. Fuck you. Fuck both of you," Bishop Wiley said aloud, before crossing his arms and rearing back in his brown leather office chair. He pointed to the computer screen. "I got you now, Babycakes." He smiled, watching the show from his office on the main level.

Neither, Monica nor Jevon knew CW was home and had just woken up from a short nap in his first floor office. If it weren't for Jevon and his emergency, he'd still be with Sugar. Now, he knew why Jevon had not showed at Café Intermezzo, or answered his cell phone. But now, because of Jevon, the bishop sat in his office recliner, hands behind his head, a clown smile plastered across his face. And if it weren't for the chirping home alarm signaling someone coming through the door, he would most likely still be asleep in his office.

He thought it was Monica entering the house, until he tuned on the surveillance system he'd installed a couple weeks ago. Things were working themselves out better than he had imagined. Now he wouldn't have to pay Jevon a dime for screwing his wife. It was just a matter of time before he had to deal with Jevon's twin, Jordan. In time, in time, he thought as he leaned back and continued watching Jevon make love to his wife.

His cell phone began buzzing.

It had to be important for someone to be calling him at four-thirty in the morning, he thought.

"Hello?" he said into his earpiece.

"I'm going to make him pay. I'm telling you, Clarence, he is mine."

"Calm down, sister. Just calm down and tell me what happened?"

"Everything was fine. I fucked him and her. You were right. I mean, you called it right on the head. He tried to act like he didn't know me. But, I played right along with him. At least until he started choking me. At first I was like yeah keep squeezing. I even had a dual orgasm, right before I passed out."

"That's what you like. Why are you so upset?"

"I ain't mad at being choked out. I'm mad cause the black motha', I mean, negro, left me on the hotel floor, him and your bitch."

"What do you mean, he left?" CW asked.

"He left. What part of left don't you understand? The negro left me for dead, just like he did six years ago. Same way I'm gon' leave him, the only difference is, his ass won't ever wake up."

"Cheryl, listen to me." He paused. "I vouched for you. I put my neck on the line getting you released in my custody. You owe it to yourself and you owe it to me—"

"Bishop, save that for them fools givin' you they hard-earned money every Sunday. I don't owe you a damn thing."

"Oh, you don't?"

"Hell nah, I don't."

"What small memories we have." He took a deep breath. "Cheryl, Cheryl, Cheryl. Have you forgotten that the only reason you're on the streets is because I told the board I'd be responsible for you?"

"So, whachu sayin'? Negro, have you forgot all the cum I swallowed back at that place. All the times I sucked your dick when you were supposed to be giving me spiritual counseling?"

"What about our agreement?" he asked.

"I'm gon' deliver, but we gon' do shit my way. The rules changed when your bitch and that mothafucka left me in that room. Oh, you better believe I'm gon' take care of Mr. Jordan Hayes."

"Let me tell you something." He sat up in his chair. "Now listen to me very closely. I don't care what happened in that room, you will not, and I repeat, you will not divert from the plan. You'll still get Jordan, but you get him where I say, and when I say. Do you understand?"

"Yeah, I understand. Uhm-hmm. I understand that you done lost your damn mind, talkin' to me like that. Nigga, I ain't your child, or your bitch. You don't run shit here, but your mouth."

"No, babycakes. I run you. And as long as I have one finger, to dial one number, I can run you right back into that nuthouse."

"You can do that. And I can't do a damn thing to stop you. Just like you can't stop me from getting this tape into the media's hands."

"What tape?" he asked.

"The tape I'm making of this very conversation, sucker."

<u>Chapter 26</u>

" *J*'m about to invent a new sucker, and I'm going to name it after you. Ho Savers."

"Man, forget you," Jordan said, waving Jevon's comments away while stretching in the grass.

Jevon looked down at his watch. "Shit, it ain't nothing but 8:15 and it's already," he looked at the temperature on the digital board at the park's entrance, "seventy-five degrees."

"Are you guys twins?" A gray-haired slim white man wearing black Speedos stopped and asked.

"No," Jevon said, shaking his head. "We just met."

"Nooo. Are you serious? You guys look just alike," the man said, bending over right in front of Jevon.

"Old man, you better get your—"

"No, we're twins," Jordan interrupted, "my brother's just joking."

"I knew it. I knew it," the man said as he rose from tying his running shoes, before hitting the jogging trail.

"I can't stand dumb-ass people and their dumb-ass questions. *Are you guys twins*," Jevon mimicked.

"The man is old, Jevon."

"So. What age gotta do with ignorance? Old ass need to be in a home or a casket."

"Jevon!"

"Don't Jevon me. I'm just keepin' it real."

Jordan put on his sun goggles. "Whachu so uptight about? Man, you been bitchin' since I picked you up this morning."

"Bullshit. I'm just tired of a perpetual cycle of bullshit. I'm tired of you."

"Me. What did I do?"

"What you always do. Judge. You always judging me like you God."

"Man, I don't judge you," Jordan said.

"I can't tell. Friday, you tripped on me steppin' out on Chey. You questioned my daddy-raising tactics. You even insinuated that I shouldn't have gone out to First Fridays."

"That's not judging. Here, help me out," Jordan said, putting his leg in Jevon's hand. "It's called love."

"I wish you'd show me a lot less love, and more understanding. Here, give me the other leg," Jevon said after stretching out Jordan's left leg. "I remember when you and I were just alike. Hell, you had ho's you fucked in shifts like a damn job."

"We're still alike. I just don't act on impulse like I used to. It's called focused control. I have to keep my eyes on the prize."

"What prize?"

"Our youth. Our young boys are messed up real bad. And I'm trying to fix what our generation has done, or shall I say has not done."

"That's what I'm saying. Man," he held out his arms in the morning sun, "enjoy life; them kids gon' be what they gon' be. You can't save the world?"

"Yeah, but I can save one. And that'll mean one less slave for the system to incarcerate. And that one, means I save a generation."

"Dog, you gotta first save yourself. Self-preservation is the first law of man."

"I am saved. Not in the Americanized commercial-Christian aspect, but my mind is clear and focused."

"Damn!" Jevon said, checking out two sisters jogging by. "You need to do some controlled focus on some new pussy."

Jordan looked at the ladies. "I ain't never said I was no saint." He started jogging. "I love me some chocolate. And I gets mine; don't worry about me."

"You used to get yours, Captain Save A Ho."

"You the only ho I'm trying to save. And tell me this," Jordan took off his T-shirt and wrapped it around his fist. "Why does every sistah have to be a ho? Why can't she be a queen, or just simply a sistah?"

"There you go with that bullshit. You went to prison, did a little time, read a couple books, and now you a holier-than-thou-Captain Save A Ho pussy prophet. Man, prison done fucked you up."

"How you figure that? I mean, just because whenever I look at a Black woman I see Momma? I see a woman who is or probably will be a mother. And if things were different, I realize the woman you call ho or bitch could have very well been our mother." Jordan shook his head. "No bruh, the nickel I served made me re-evaluate my life and my value system. I dialogued with some old heads that got me to see shit I've always taken for granted. I started reading about struggle, and I saw that my shit was gravy compared to what others before me had gone through, especially sistahs."

"Come on, dog, I ain't trying to hear that, not for-real for real, "Jevon said. "You still fuck ho's."

Jordan looked at his watch. "Speed up." Jordan looked down at his stop watch. "It took four minutes on the first half mile."

A minute later Jordan continued. "Yeah, I get my groove on, but I'm always straight up with a sistah. I don't pull no punches or play games. I let them know up front that I'm not looking for anything more than a friend, but if something more comes out of it, well, that's all good."

"And that makes you better than me?"

"No, I never said that. I know I ain't living right, but at least I'm giving the sistah the choice to deal with my shit or go on and try and find someone that is looking for the same things she is." Jordan turned around and jogged backward jabbing a finger in his chest. "And I don't screw married women."

Jevon sped up, turned around and jogged backward. "Ladies, you are looking dashing this morning," he said to the women they had seen earlier. "Look at those asses. Them ho's don't need to walk, they need me up in that ass. I'm all the exercise they'll need."

Jordan just shook his head.

Jevon continued. "You missing out, bruh. Married women are less drama. I won't say *no* drama, but I will say less."

"Man, that's just bad karma," Jordan said, running up the steep mountain's hill near the three-mile mark.

"Slow the fuck down, man. Shit, I can't talk and keep this pace up," Jevon said as they ran up another hill.

"I'm trying to finish in under forty minutes," Jordan said. "You know I have to pick up Ariel by ten."

"Oh, I forgot."

"You should go with us, come hear me speak. You need God in your life."

"I got God in my life, and I appreciate all the pussy He endows me with. Besides, I ain't trying to hear that jungle oom-gaba-oom-baba ancestral shit you talk about at that church."

"I know, that's why you should go. Get back to your roots, find out who you are and understand what your mission in life is."

"I know what my mission is."

"I'm scared to ask."

"Since you are, I'll go ahead and tell you," Jevon said.

"I was afraid of that."

"It's simple. Fuck 'em, before they fuck you. And most important, if they can't do anything for you, then don't go back for seconds."

"That is sad."

"Sad? Ain't shit sad about busting a nut. It ain't like I'm selling drugs, getting high, or robbing folks. I'm just getting pussy, and besides, I make my ho's feel good, so I'm giving back to the community in my own way. A few times, I even fucked a three-in-the-morning, last-piece-of-pussy-in-the-club ho, in the daytime. If that ain't charity, I don't know what is."

They were coming up on the fourth mile. Jordan neglected to tell him that he was speaking at Beautiful Baptist this morning instead of First Afrikan, because that would have opened up a whole new can of worms. Besides, he wouldn't come either way, so Jordan left well enough alone.

Jevon thought Jordan didn't know, but thanks to his three-year-old niece, Jordan knew that his brother had some sort of relationship with Bishop Wiley. One he planned to get to the bottom of.

"Running out of gas, superstar?" Jevon said, racing in front of his brother.

"Never that," Jordan said, kicking it into another gear.

While coming around a curve heading for the point where they'd begun, Jordan thought about how at peace he was and how lost Jevon was. The man was paid. He and his wife owned a half-million-dollar home. He had the most beautiful, intelligent baby girl on the planet. He was married to a queen of queens. He'd even made his own fortune parlaying his wife's money in real estate. And after all that, he was still prowling the streets looking for a greater happiness, like a drug addict looking for the ultimate high.

Not one day in the four and a half years he had spent behind bars did he ever regret taking the rap for Jevon. Jordan knew prison would devour his brother, like it had done so many other weak souls. They may have shared the same looks, but their hearts couldn't be more different. Even in school, or just growing up in the projects, no one messed with Jevon, because they couldn't be sure it wasn't Jordan.

School was easy. Too easy for Jevon. He could have been or done anything he wanted, but he was lazy, always trying to take shortcuts, getting over on folks. And Jordan was always there to fight his brother's battles.

"Time?" Jevon asked with his hands on his knees."

"Thirty-nine minutes and forty-one seconds."

"Who's your daddy, boy?" Jevon said triumphantly before falling to the grass, where they began stretching.

"I'm so tired, I can't even enjoy running rings around that ass," Jevon said, between breaths. "You gon' have to carry me to the car, Jordan. I can't move."

Jordan was bent over, hands on his knees. "The only place I'm carrying you is to church. After the way you're screwing over Cheyenne, you need some spiritual upliftment."

"Uplift these nuts," he said, grabbing his crotch.

"Watch your mouth. I'll still put my foot up your ass."

"And that'll be the last day you see the sun rise. I ain't the man I used to be, Jordan. And you gon' quit handlin' me any old kind a'way," Jevon said, rising to his knees.

"No need to get mad at me. I'm not the one with a wife and kid at home and out fucking my wife's best friend."

He pointed a finger at Jordan. "That's exactly why I don't tell you shit anymore."

"What, you mean like what you got goin' on with that shady used car salesman? The Bishop you in business with."

"Damn, dog, you just hatin' for no reason at all this morning," he said, walking toward Stone Mountain Park's entrance. "When it comes to my shit, your jealous ass, just loves to hate."

Jordan shouted at Jevon's back. "Bishop Wiley got you so confused; you can't even differentiate love from hate."

Chapter 27

*O*h, the hate. For the last three years she had to put up with the snobbish deacons' wives. They had her pegged as a gold-digger. The old crust-bucket haters were just mad because she dug for gold and hit a diamond mine. If they only knew what hell their good bishop had reigned on her, they'd be humming a different tune, Monica thought. One even called her a floozy, to which she kindly told the old no-tooth antique to go kill herself and make the world a better place.

She couldn't help that she was twenty-eight and the Bishop was forty-five. The old biddies had to take that up with God. But the old busy-body biddies were part of the reason she loved Sunday mornings. It had nothing at all to do with church. Hell, church was a business. It was work, and being the First Lady required much more than she had expected, but the benefits well outweighed the shortcomings, Monica thought while their driver opened the car's back door.

"Thank you, Brother James," Bishop Wiley said after getting out behind Monica.

"Bishop Wiley, Bishop Wiley," several members cried out.

Bishop Wiley blocked out the Sunday morning sun with one hand while he smiled and waved for the parishioners that hadn't made it in before their arrival. After he and Monica made their entrance, the others would be escorted into the church auditorium balcony.

"I don't see why you have to dress like that, woman. This is a place of worship not the Hip Hop Music awards," the Bishop said under his breath, as he walked hand in hand, escorting Monica up the mountain of stairs that led to the humongous Beautiful Baptist church vestibule.

"No, you ain't talkin'." She stopped on a middle stair.

He smiled as he spoke through clinched teeth. "Woman, don't make a scene. Not here, not now."

She too smiled at the church members and guests that stood to the left and to the right of the purple and gold awning that covered the walkway and stairs. "You make a scene every Sunday, having a driver drive us up front in your four-hundred-thousand-dollar Benz." She could care less about him, but not really wanting to make a scene, she continued walking up the stairs.

"It's five hundred, and it's a Maybach."

Once inside the dome-like vestibule, Bishop Wiley took out a small mirror as he did every Sunday, while the church benediction was being read. He checked to make sure there wasn't a hair out of place, his tailored suit was void of any wrinkles or lint, and his gators had no scuffs on them.

"I bet that cross around your neck is bigger and has more diamonds in it than Nelly's," Monica whispered.

"Nelly's?" he replied.

"The rapper. The one that did *Tip Drill*, a few years back."

He just shook his head as the twenty-foot castle-like, center-aisle oak double doors electronically opened. The church orchestra's percussion section started its drum roll. The dry ice machine produced a thick fog, preventing anyone from seeing the Bishop and his young wife.

Reverend C. Webb, one of the junior ministers stood behind the podium. "Let me read you a passage from the book of Jeremiah." He put a pair of horn rimmed glasses on his face. "Jeremiah thirty, twenty-first verse: Their leader will be one of their own; their ruler will arise from among them. I will bring him near and he will come close to me." The short, big-belly, middle-aged, dark-skinned junior minister paused. He banged his fist on the podium. Several octaves higher and louder, he continued with a finger pointed up in the air. "For who is he who will devote himself to be close to Me?"

Bishop Wiley emerged from the fog, in the rear of the church.

"It is he," the junior minister pointed to the back of the church. "Our precious lord has delivered among us, a disciple of His grace, His glory, His benevolence; I give you the Bishop C. Wendell Wiley and First Lady Monica Monique Wiley."

All three levels of the amphitheatre-like concert hall church was on its feet applauding.

Bishop Wiley hid his embarrassment well as he did every Sunday, as he and Monica walked down the red carpeted middle aisle. Why couldn't she dress like a First Lady? he wondered.

Monica smiled and waved, as she strutted down the aisle wearing a sunshine-orange Versace form-fitting mid-cut dress, orange stockings, and brown Dolce & Gabana open-toe heels that matched the Prada scarf and the hourglass Gaultier sunglasses that covered her eyes.

The Angels of Faith concert choir sang the word *walk* repeatedly, as the two came forward and stepped onto the electronic lift that rose, bringing them up onto the stage.

Monica could hardly wait to smile at the twenty-seven ancient wives of the deacons as she made her way to the First Lady's throne in the center of the concert-like stage.

Haters. They would've been successful if I hadn't been planning our marriage since before the first time we met, Monica thought as she took her seat.

Every light in the church went dim. Every light that is, except the spotlight, which was on the Bishop.

The church was still. Every eye was focused on Bishop Wiley. He raised his arms above his head. His stare went from the congregation to the stained-glass dome ceiling. Suddenly a loud burst of thunder erupted inside the church walls.

The congregation gasped.

"Praise the Lord! For all who fear God and trust in Him are blessed beyond expression. Yes, happy is the man who delights in doing his commands. He himself shall be wealthy, and his good deeds will never be forgotten. Psalms 112: 1-3." His voice was amplified over the one hundred speakers surrounding the church compound.

It had cost the church nearly two hundred thousand dollars for the lights, sound effects and the custom-designed podium that doubled as a control station. But it was worth every penny, just like his mentor and confidante, Bishop TJ Money had told him.

Wild Cherry

After pressing a button on the podium, the lights dimmed. "Now, family, as we know, the wisest, I said the wisest man in the Bible wrote Psalms, am I right?"

"Yes sir, Bishop!" Behind him, Deacon Jacobs spoke out.

"Sho, ya right?" someone in the front row shouted.

"Now, let me help you understand what God was saying when he bestowed this message unto Solomon." He began to run in place and shake his head like a boxer preparing for a prize fight.

"Preach!" came another voice from the congregation.

As quickly as he began running, he stopped. With one hand, Bishop Wiley pointed to the cloud-and-sky colored stained glass ceiling and with the other, he hit the button on the podium that paged his choir conductor. "For those who praise Him," he said.

On cue, the choir sang the words, "Praise Him."

Again the lights dimmed and the spotlight was back on him. "For those who," Bishop Wiley pointed a finger to the ceiling. "Praise Him."

The spotlight jumped to the choir. "Praise Him," they sang.

"Praise Him," he said.

"Praise Him," the choir sang.

They went back and forth like this for a good two minutes before the congregation joined in, singing the words "Praise Him."

Moments later, the church lights went black and the spotlight shone on the bishop and the podium.

The church was silent. Bishop Wiley's eyes were closed. Two fingers touched his lips as he looked to be in prayer. Seconds later, the church lights came back on after he opened his eyes and placed both hands on the podium.

"The scripture I just read is simple. How much plainer can it get? Scripture reads, If you praise God," he shot a hand in the air, "and trust in Him, not your boyfriend, girlfriend, wife, husband, mother, father, or even me-trust in Him." He banged a fist on the corner of the podium. "And only Him, you are blessed. Blessed beyond expression." He pointed to the congregation. "Listen to me, family. God said..." He paused. "I don't think y'all hear me now." He threw both hands in the air. "I said, God said, you are blessed beyond expression. That means words can't describe how bountifully blessed you are."

A middle-aged, heavyset woman stood up and hollered, "Yes, Lawd! Yes, Lawd! Praise Him! Praise his Holy name! Thank you, Jesus, Thank you, Jesus."

Louder and with more passion, the bishop continued, "Happy is the man who delights in doing His commands. He himself shall be wealthy, and his deeds will never be forgotten."

He brought his hand down, grabbed the microphone, and walked away from the podium and over to the lift. The bishop descended from the stage, to be more intimate with the thousands of faces that decorated the church's main level.

He put the palm of his hand on his chest. "I own a four-million-dollar home. I've recently purchased a fifteen-million dollar private jet, and I drive around town in a half million-dollar car. The naysayers call me the pimp in the pulpit, Player Preacher, Black Caesar, and I'm sure most of you have heard other names."

"I love you, Bishop," a young lady shouted from the middle aisle, front row.

The pretty little thing was blessed with a body that'll make a gay man go straight, he thought before replying, "I love you, too, sweetie." Uhm, uhm, uhm. Lord Jesus, give me strength. Good Lord, this little piece of fruit was fine, he thought, making a mental note to see about getting her into a one-on-one counseling session in the near future.

He continued. "I'm here to testify before you today, family. As your brother in Christ, Bishop C. Wendell Wiley." He paused. "I Love Him. Praise Him. Fear Him." Shaking his head he continued. "And I trust only in Him." He closed his eyes, embraced himself, and smiled. "And I'm ecstatic, excited, and more than delighted in serving Him."

"Praise Jesus," someone shouted.

He opened his eyes and said, "For my loyalty, my Father has rewarded me with wealth as He told Solomon He would. He has blessed me beyond expression. So who are they that cast stones but dwellers of glass houses? Those same stones will boomerang and shatter the very foundations from which their stones were cast."

The lights went out, and a streak of what looked like lightning struck the brown Bible the bishop held in the air.

A moment later, the spotlight came on and was shining on the bishop. "For God is my rock." He smiled. "My force field. He shields me. Not even lightening can harm me as long as God's arms are wrapped around me. So those that stand in judgment of me beware, for God's wrath is mighty and it comes without warning."

He backed up and stepped back onto the lift. Back on the stage he glanced at his watch. A half hour left. He smiled at the cutie that pledged her love to him moments ago. His member rose under his purple and gold robe just thinking of the counsel he'd like to give her.

He smiled at one of the naysayers he'd tricked into coming to today's service.

Jordan Hayes was a thorn in his finger, one that was beginning to fester and expand. That's why he had to show the congregation that he, Bishop C. Wendell Wiley, was the bigger man, and at the same time he had to put Jordan and everyone like him in their places.

Jordan didn't realize that if the bishop really wanted to crush him, he could. The only reason he didn't was because of Jevon, and the timing.

All he had to do was show Cherry that Jevon wasn't Jordan, but he couldn't, at least not yet. It had already taken Jevon upwards of a year to get his wife into bed. Now that he had, he would now begin the process of getting rid of her, and Cherry would get rid of Jevon, so he'd be the sole owner of the new Conyers City Center Mall. Jevon must've been a fool to think for $250,000 in bank robbery money that he'd have a twenty percent stake in His and the Bishop TJ Money's Christian mall development project. Everything was working out better than he'd planned.

"Today, I've invited some of my biggest critics to speak to you, family," the bishop said.

Boos loudly resounded from the congregation.

"Now, now," the bishop held out his arms to calm the congregation. "Family, you know I've always said that I'm far from perfect, and I do make mistakes." He extended his arm in back of him toward Jordan. "Obviously, Mr. Hayes thinks I'm a terror, as he calls it, I'm pimping the black community and," he smiled, "you, my beautiful brothers and sisters of Beautiful Baptist."

Again a staccato of boos resounded louder than they had at first.

"Please, family, please," the bishop pleaded. "Let's give him the floor, let him speak directly to you. Let's give

Mr. Jordan Hayes a warm round of applause," the bishop said, clapping his hands.

"That Hayes boy needs Jesus," a church member shouted.

"Need to look in the mirror. Using our Bishop to get media attention," another shouted.

"Damn you, boy," another shouted as Jordan took the microphone.

Bishop Wiley took his seat next to his wife. He patted her hand thinking how good it would be to have his hands wrapped around the handle of a gun tapping the barrel against her hard head as she begged for her life. He wore a wide smile on his face just thinking that at the end of Monica's cries and pleas, it would be him pulling the trigger.

Chapter 28

*J*t would be so easy to pull the trigger. Just do it, girl. Lift up the covers, put your free hand in the slit of his boxers, pull out his penis, put the barrel right up to the head and *bang*.

If it were only that easy, she thought while staring at her husband's naked frame, sleeping peacefully under the white Egyptian, silk sheets. Cheyenne turned and looked at the clock hanging above the sixty-inch plasma TV built inside the wall in front of the bed.

It was four in the morning. The recurring nightmare of that night in the park with Jevon had awoken her. Although she had awakened in a cold sweat, she still hit the remote on the nightstand built into the wall to her left, slowing the platinum, stainless-steel blades of the three fans that hung from the ceiling in the middle of the bedroom.

She didn't know if it was the cold, white marble floor, anticipation, or fear that had her trembling as she climbed off of the platform that their bed rested on in the middle of the huge bedroom.

Wild Cherry

Although the room was chilly, the gray sweats and the white wifebeater tank she had on were damp with perspiration. This must have been the twentieth time she'd stood over him, gun in hand, pointed at his crotch while he slept. And each time her eyes burned with tears of hate and rage. If it weren't for her daughter, and the undying love she had for her husband's twin, she wouldn't blink twice before pulling the trigger.

She'd earned her doctorate and was making well into six figures before the age of twenty-seven. At thirty-three, she was fit, healthy, married, and owned a half-million dollar dream home she'd let her husband build from the ground up. Anyone looking in from the outside would think she was blessed, but she knew oh too well that her success proved to be a curse. One that had her teetering between sanity and insanity, which was ironic because she worked with men and women who were suffering with similar forms of depression and self-loathing. Unlike her patients, she knew what her problem was and she knew how to get rid of it, but that meant a long stint in prison, losing her daughter and losing hope of being with the only man she'd ever loved.

Hate couldn't even begin to describe the way she felt about the man that had blackmailed and tricked her into marrying him. And she couldn't blame Jordan for being so robotic around her. Why Jordan couldn't see who is brother really was, was beyond her comprehension. What did Jordan think of his brother marrying her? Why didn't he ever call her from prison?

To this day, she couldn't understand why Jevon got her pregnant and married her. He could've gotten anything he wanted from her without marriage and he knew that. She would have given him over one-hundred thousand dollars cash, every cent she had at that time, if he would've just disappeared from her life.

Love was her downfall. It was her own fault. Six years ago she met a man, sort of a patient. She was moonlighting as a Narcotics Anonymous group counselor then. It was a part-time gig. It was in one of those sessions when their eyes introduced themselves. Such passion, she'd thought, as his hazel brown orbs melted her heart.

Against her better judgment, she went after him. She'd followed him for several blocks. A man with morals, she thought as she watched him turn down an opportunity to sleep with an attractive white woman. A man who cared, she thought as she later watched him hold a conversation with, and give money to a homeless man. And after walking up on him, her heart danced. Unconsciously he touched her hand as they joked with each other on the late night downtown Atlanta streets. It only took him touching her that one time for her to know. No one had ever sparked so many emotions in her at one time, she'd thought.

For the next few hours, they'd walked and talked about anything and everything. He was passionate, sincere, remorseful, and he wanted so much more for his brother and others.

The vibrant conversation they had shared that night seemed to make the streetlights shine brighter. Even the humming of car engines that passed seemed melodic, in tune with all the night noise heard on an Atlanta downtown, that Thursday night.

For four hours they had basked in each other's company, holding hands, laughing, talking, listening, and just enjoying moments of sweet silence together. Before the end of the evening she was sure, without a doubt, recovering drug addict or not, this man was her soulmate.

She remembered feeling like a silly teenager the next day at work, picking up the phone and dialing a couple of digits before hanging up. She'd done this several times throughout the day. She'd checked her cell phone every chance she got, hoping that somehow she'd missed his call. And when it did ring, she prayed it was him. Around three in the afternoon, after not hearing from him, she had pressed star sixty-seven to block out her number before she'd dialed the number he'd given her.

When his voicemail picked up, she sighed, before leaving the first of several unreturned messages.

She couldn't get him or that night off of her mind. She'd never gone after a man. They'd always pursued her, and at first she had no intention of doing what she had done. Although she had access to patient records, their personal profiles were off limits.

That's why it took her so long to build up the courage to pull up Jordan's file.

Two weeks after they'd met, she stood outside of the basement apartment where he lived, according to the records she'd pulled.

What would he say? Was he really married? Did he lie about not having children? Had that entire evening been a lie? All these and so many other wild thoughts had ran through her mind, before she smoothed out her cream colored skirt and built up the courage to knock on the door.

Once he opened the door, the first thing she had noticed was his eyes. They were different. Dull and lifeless, she'd thought. The thought had never occurred to her that Jordan had a twin; that was one thing that Jordan had left out of their long conversation. He'd talked about his brother, but he'd never said he was a twin.

Not long after she'd entered the apartment, Jevon had poured on the charm, and in no time she felt at ease.

"Why didn't you call? Why didn't you come back to group?" She had asked.

"I couldn't." He'd shook his head. "I just couldn't bare to see you again, knowing that there was no way there could be an *us*. The *us* I'd dreamed of every night, since that special night."

"I don't understand," she had said.

He lightly touched the back of her hand. "I'm a drug addict. I have nothing. Nothing to offer you. And you have so much. You deserve so much more than I can give. It's just not fair to you."

That's when the first of many tears to come fell from her eyes. "Jordan, you're wrong." She'd shaken her head. "Oh. But you are so wrong." She sniffed, looking him in his eyes. "It's not about what you have or where you've been. It's what you do from here. Where you go. And Jordan, right now, I just want to ride on your wave," she'd said.

The next evening they had met on the boardwalk at Piedmont Park, in midtown Atlanta. She remembered walking up to him and thinking that his whole demeanor seemed different. Sort of cocky yet reserved, much more aggressive-looking.

She had lightened up and let her guard down when from behind his back he brought forth a large brown wooden picnic basket, with a blue blanket folded up on the top. She remembered smiling, thinking this was the man she'd fell for that late night, weeks ago. The summer sun had not long ago faded into the Sunday night sky. She remembered thinking that it had been so romantic.

Wild Cherry

They'd dined on peanut butter and jelly sandwiches, Pringles potato chips, and Concord grape juice. His back was against a large oak tree overlooking a dark pond. Cheyenne was at ease, lying on his lap listening to the wind sing and watching the leaves dance in the invisible night breeze.

She had trusted him and she needed him to trust her. Her counseling experience led her to believe he was holding back. At times his conversation seemed scripted. His body language didn't match his words, she'd remembered. She should have taken heed to the signs, but, she was consumed with want. Wanting him to relax and open up to her superseded twelve years of training and counseling.

In hopes of getting him to open up, she began speaking about her own past personal experience with drug addiction. Only God, and her girl, Monica knew about her drug problem before she opened up to Jevon.

Tears streamed down her face as she stood over the bed, gun in hand, remembering. Remembering how difficult it had been opening up, telling Jevon of her pain. The story about how she'd started off taking Percosets and Valiums to relax, study, and work the long hours she had while in med school. She explained how she'd written her own prescriptions, forging physicians' names while studying. And how, by the time she'd graduated from Meharry, came back to Atlanta and completed her intern residency in Grady Hospital's suicide ward. Cheyenne couldn't get through a few hours, let alone a shift, without her meds.

The most painful part of revealing her soul to Jevon, was telling him about Sadaka Simon. Cheyenne was working a twenty-four-hour shift. And she was high as a

junkie on payday when, halfway into her shift, Sadaka's
mother had burst into Grady's ER screaming and fighting
to drag her daughter through the glass double doors.

By the look of mother and daughter, you didn't know
who was injured. Blood and sweat had been all over the
both of them. They both were screaming. The mother tried
to restrain her wildly kicking and fighting daughter.

"I hate you ! I hate me! Let me die! And if you don't
I'll find a way! I don't wanna be me! I won't be me!" the
little girl had said over and over. Cheyenne, being the only
psychiatrist available at the time, had never seen anything
like it. She'd studied similar cases in medical school, but
reading and seeing it were two completely different things.
It was as if the little girl was possessed, like a black Linda
Blair in the movie *The Exorcist*. Even after several
members of the hospital staff were able to get the girl onto
a restraining bed, Sadaka fought like hell to break through
the restraints around her bleeding ankles and wrists.

High and in a panic, Cheyenne accidentally
administered an IV drip filled with an amphetamine. An
hour later the little girl went into cardiac arrest and died.

Ms. Simon was so devastated that she never even
thought to have Cheyenne investigated. And the hospital
board never batted an eye in Cheyenne's direction.

Cheyenne remembered taking Jevon's hand in the park
and squeezing it so hard, she felt him wince in pain. She
kept that grip while saying, "I made a pledge after that little
girl died, that I'd dedicate my life to helping drug addicts
like myself and young people suffering from depression."

Not long after she had bared her soul, Cheyenne and
Jevon shared a passionate kiss and against her wishes, he
rolled over on top of her. Although she had given herself to
him the day before, when she showed up at his apartment,

this time something just didn't feel right. She looked into his eyes and it was then that she knew she'd made a big mistake.

He had her arms and legs pinned to the ground. The black night and the large oak they were under shielded anyone from seeing them. He was too big, too strong; there was no need to struggle, she knew his type. Struggling only aroused rapists and made them more violent. She'd evaluated and counseled rapists and victims in the past. She never imagined that one day she'd be a victim herself.

All his weight was on her as he managed to pull his sweats down to his knees. He reached under the cute tennis skirt she wore, grabbed her panties and yanked, ripping them off in one swift motion. Next, he forced himself inside her.

It had been so painful. She'd been dry. Only God heard her silent cries as he started slow and hard. Jevon lifted her legs and bent them back past her forehead before pounding himself in and out of her so fast and with so much force, she had thought she was going to pass out from the pain.

What Jevon had said after he rolled off of her had shocked her almost as much as the rape had.

"In the Dekalb County Jail visiting room, the day after Jordan was arrested he couldn't shut up talking about you. He went on and on about this angel he'd met. I mean you should've heard him. He made you sound as if you were something from a black fairy tale. I never heard my brother speak about anyone like he had about you. So, of course, I knew that if given the chance I had to have this forbidden fruit he'd spoke of," Jevon had said.

Jevon got a kick out of telling Cheyenne things that he knew she wouldn't repeat. Things like he'd made the anonymous call to the Dekalb County Police telling them that Jordan had robbed the bank to support his crack habit, and he went on to tell them where Jordan lived. He'd done all this from his car in the apartment complex parking lot after he sent Sunny into the apartment building.

If Cheyenne ever breathed a word to Jordan, Jevon had threatened to tell the police everything she'd told him about Sadaka Simon's death.

Cheyenne had offered Jevon money, sex, and even her condo, anything to leave her alone. He'd said that there was only one thing to make him leave her alone; a baby. He had told her that if she gave him a baby, then he'd be out of her life for good.

Desperate, not wanting to go to prison, and wanting to get him out of her life, she reluctantly agreed.

Now, standing over the bed, tears free-falling from her face, gun pointed at him, she could not believe how naïve and stupid she'd been to agree to his terms. By the time she'd had his baby, she was numb. She was content to live the rest of her life as a robot, with no feeling for anything or anyone. But, after giving birth to and holding the little brown baby in her arms, a tsunami of love overwhelmed her. But the feeling was short lived and replaced by hate. Undying hate for the man who'd forced her into bringing an innocent child into the world. And a deep determination not to let him have her baby.

Of course this was never his plan. After the baby came, he again threatened to go to the police if she didn't marry him.

And now, six years later, she stood over Jevon, his loaded .38 in her steady hand. "I should blow the head of your penis clean off," she whispered.

Jordan and Ariel were so close. Ariel loved the ground Jordan walked on. He'd take care of her. He'd raise her baby with all the love and care in the world. Cheyenne had a trust fund already set up for Ariel's college education. Everything would be all right. She smiled before pulling the hammer back on the shiny gun.

Chapter 29

"*W*ho's your daddy? Huh?" *Pop*. He asked while smacking that ass with a stainless-steel spatula.

"You are, poppy. Ooooohhh. Fuck me, poppy, harder, po-ppppppy. Give it to me, poppa-choolohhh," Meila cooed.

"Feel me, babygirl. Ooh shit," he said. "I want you to feel all nine-point-three inches of crooked dick up in that ass."

"Poppy! Oh poppy! I feel it! I feel it! Harder! Harder!" The eighteen-year-old high school senior shouted.

There wasn't anything like low-mileage young tight, wet Puerto Rican pussy, he thought. "Oh, you want Big Daddy to hurt that pussy?" He grabbed hold of the sink's stainless-steel nozzle and pushed her in the middle of her back, causing her to be bent over the kitchen sink.

Jevon could see his house from the window over Meila's sink. While he slowly long stroked, driving his manhood in out and all around, hitting all four of her inner walls, Meila's butter-brown 36 C's were bouncing around, making suds in the fresh dishwater.

162

"Harder, poppy! Harder!" she shouted.

Jevon grabbed her waist, stood straight up and lurched forward with all the force he could muster.

"Ahhhhhh poooo-tow!" she shouted, cursing in her native tongue.

"What's my name, got dammit? What's my motha fuckin' name, be-otch?" he asked as he slapped her ass and pounded in and out of the high school girl that he'd fantasized about since the girl and her family moved in across the street, a year ago.

All of a sudden, her head spun around. "Who the fuck cares what your name is?" she said in a voice deeper than Barry White's.

"Oh shit? What the? Who in hell?" Jevon said backing into a table.

"Nobody cares what your name is. No matter how hard you try, you will never be your brother," Meila shouted, walking backward toward him with a clown-like smile on her face. As she spoke, hair grew from her chin and upper lip. Her face began to wrinkle and her hair fell out in clumps. "Who's your daddy now, bitch?" she asked.

"Noooooooo!" he shouted, while reaching out and grabbing her arm.

"Ahhhh, yeah, suck it, gay boy," she said.

He looked at the arm he'd grabbed. "Ahhhhhhh!" he screamed, noticing the arm had turned into a huge penis with long straight hair and a mustache around the tip. He pulled and jerked, but his hand was stuck to the large penis.

The more he pulled, the more the thing in front of him became aroused. "Put it in your mouth," the man who a minute ago was an eighteen-year-old girl, said.

"Nooo," he screamed, lurching up from the bed, scaring Cheyenne.

Her vibrating cell phone caused her to instinctively turn her head toward her nightstand.

He blinked a couple times, his heart pounding, realizing he'd had a nightmare, and recognizing that what he'd awoke to was a living nightmare. He used the cell phone distraction to lurch forward and grab her arm.

"Let me go!" Cheyenne shouted.

"What the fuck? Bitch, whachu' gon' do with my gun?"

"Let me go!" She jerked and twisted.

She dropped the gun on the floor as he jerked her arm, pulling her onto the bed. "Bitch, you was gon' shoot me?"

"No, I *am* going to shoot you," she said, wrestling to get away so she could go for the gun.

He swung her over his body to the other side of the bed. Cheyenne's long Barack Obama T-shirt was around her waist as she kicked and squirmed. The grip around her waist was immoveable.

He stuck his tongue in her ear. "Before you shoot me, you know, I'm gon' have ta tap that ass. See how you like it up the ass, bitch," he said.

"Never. You child molester. It's bad enough you fuck anything in a skirt, but that girl across the street is in high school."

"Ah, woman I was having a damn dream. I mean, a nightmare," he said, sliding to the side, trying to get Cheyenne on her back. "I can't believe you was gon' try to shoot me."

"I don't know why. I hate you! I hate you!" she screamed then banged her head into his face.

He grabbed his nose. "Bitch, you broke my nose."

She jumped off the bed and slipped off the platform before falling onto the white marble floor. "You gon' die this Sunday morning, asshole," she shouted, regaining her balance.

"Who the fuck! Who the fuck you think you talkin' too?" he said running behind her. "Come'ere, woman." He dove for her.

She fell to the ground in the upstairs hallway. "Let my leg go!" she shouted as she kicked and squirmed.

"On everything I love, I promise, when I'm finished with you, you gon' respect me. I'm still the dick in this damn house."

She grabbed the leg of the stand that her Thomas Blackshear porcelain figurine collection rested on. "Let me go," she screamed, as he pulled her toward him. The stand broke, and the porcelain collection went tumbling everywhere. She just barely managed to grab a foot-long figurine of an older black man, speaking to a group of young boys.

"I own you, bitch."

"Own this," she said sending the porcelain figurine flying through the air.

He let go of her leg. "Shit!" He hollered, putting a hand to his eye. "You tried to put my eye out."

She ran down their spiral staircase with him on her heels. He caught up with her at the bottom. A deep cut had opened right under his eye. Blood was all over his face and chest. He picked her up and slammed her on the foyer floor. Her head made a loud thudding sound, as it hit the hardwood floor.

Moments later she woke up with him on top, ripping her panties off. "You haven't given me any since Jordan got out four months ago in February. You fuckin' my brother? Huh, bitch? Huh?" he slapped her upside the head.

"Woman, you still my wife. This my pussy for life. Understand me, bitch?"

She was in shock. *This can't be happening again. Please, God no.*

He slapped her hard across the face. "Turn over, bitch."

She was in pain. She had no idea how bad she was hurt. Her mind drifted back to the night in the park. The night she didn't fight back. "Never again!" she said slowly and clearly.

"What, bitch?" he held his hand up in a backslapping gesture.

"Ahhhhhhhhhhhhhhhh!" she screamed, bucked and turned. He reached behind himself, bracing his hands on the floor.

That was all the time and space she needed to bring a knee up.

"My dick." He grabbed his crotch. "Shit! Shit! Shit! He rolled over onto his side. "You crazy ass bitch. I was... Come back here." She was slow in getting up. Too slow. Again, he managed to grab her leg.

"Not in me! Not on me! Not around me! Never again will you or your nasty penis touch me."

"Oh, yes the fuck I and it will," he said dragging her to him, one hand still on his crotch.

She gritted her teeth. "You have to kill me first," she said, bringing her arm around and raking her nails down the side of his face.

"Got damn, motherfuck!" he cried, temporarily forgetting the pain in his crotch. He put both hands to his scratched up face.

She got up and ran into the kitchen. Her eyes focused on the key rack next to the sub-zero refrigerator.

"You leave this house and as God is my witness, I'm gon' kill you," he said, still trying to recover from the knee to his groin.

With only a long T-shirt on, she stood at the door leading to the garage. "Why should I leave? This is my house. I pay the mortgage. I had it built. No," she said, looking at the collection of knives and meat cleavers inside the glass kitchen cabinet. She had lived in fear for far too long. It's time. Past time that she faced her fears. She looked at the knife cabinet again, focusing her attentions on the single stainless-steel ice-pick. *I could kill him but he'd win,* she thought while turning and heading back into the den.

She'd been sitting on the edge of the eight-foot granite fountain on the opposite side of the wall-to-wall fireplace, for about ten minutes before Jevon limped into the room.

He looked like a boxer on the losing end of a championship fight. He had on a blue velour Phat Farm sweat suit. His nose was swollen. His eyes were red and the left side of his face was scratched up pretty bad. He placed a hand on the wall of glass that overlooked the pool and the tennis court in the backyard.

"You still here, bitch?"

"Jevon, I'm sorry God didn't make you a woman. I really am."

"Say, say what, bitch?"

"A woman. It's obvious that you degrade women so as to make yourself feel like you'd be better at being a woman than a real woman."

He frowned. "What? That shit don't even make sense."

Ignoring him, with her legs crossed, she continued, "The reason Jordan is such a better man than you are is because he *is* a man. A real man. You on the other hand are suffering from Gender Misidentification Syndrome."

"Huh?"

She uncrossed her legs and stood up. "You look like a man. You talk like a man, but, on the inside, you're a woman."

He was in a considerable amount of pain. He wanted so bad to snatch her up, and knock her teeth in her throat, but he couldn't chance it. She'd been downstairs too long. Long enough for him to go up and throw on a sweat suit and get the DVD. She could have left. And she was sitting there so calm. *No, she had something up her sleeve. She was waiting for me to attack.*

"Look at your life." She extended her hand. "Jordan has always been the athletic one. He's always been the protector, the bread winner. All manly behavior. And you've been..." she paused, "How can I say this?" She shrugged her shoulders and nodded her head. "You've been the bitch."

He laughed. "You oughta' know that psychobabble shit don't work with me. You of all bitches know I'm one-hundred percent, grade A, certified man." He grabbed his crotch. "Ouch," he said.

"You threatened to penetrate my rectum—"

"That wasn't a threat. That was a promise."

"As I was saying before you so rudely interrupted, your obsession with anal sex is typical among Gender Misidentification Syndrome." She got up and took a couple steps.

Unconsciously, he took a step back.

"You see, there is no difference in man and woman when it comes to that part of the human anatomy, which verifies your hidden desire to have relations with a man.

You probably already have. Has a man penetrated you, Jevon?"

"Fuck you!"

"Fuck you is not an answer to my question."

"I'm a man, bitch." He patted his chest. "I'm a real man," he said, his voice rising a few octaves.

"Who are you trying to convince, me or yourself?

"Fuck you, Cheyenne! You see this?" he said producing a compact disc from the pants pocket of his sweats.

They stood, eight, nine feet apart.

"As for the nasty little whores you say that I'm fucking," he smiled, holding the compact disc in the air, "I happen to have one of the nasty little whores on this DVD, one that I think you may want to see. Then again," he shrugged, "maybe you won't want to see it," he said, throwing the DVD at her.

She dodged, letting the disc slide on the hardwood floor until it banged against the fountain wall.

"My keys?" He took a step toward her.

She didn't miss, hitting him in the nose with a set of keys.

"Shit!" he shouted, grabbing his nose. "I swear ta God, you gon' make me kill you."

"Not if I kill you first?"

"You threatening me?" he asked. "Have you forgotten the little piece of information that I have? You know, the info that will put you away for a very long time."

"No, I have not." She said, smiling. "And no I am not threatening you. I am, too, making you a promise."

"What promise?" he asked walking toward the door.

"Put your hands on me again and I'll show you."

"Fuck you," he said.

"No, fuck *with* me, that's what you do Jevon Tavarus Hayes," she said right before he slammed the door leading to the garage.

Cheyenne first went back up to her bedroom to get her cell phone. She looked to see who the missed call was from earlier. She didn't notice the number. She looked at the time on the phone. 1:30. Thirty minutes later, Ariel and Jevon will be getting out of church, she thought before she pressed re-dial, and headed back down the stairs and into the theatre room to see what was on the DVD.

Chapter 30

" *I* don't claim to have all the answers when it comes to walking with the Lord." He extended an arm behind him, toward the throne that the Bishop sat on. "Bishop Wiley is by far more knowledgeable when it comes to the *Word* than I am, and probably more knowledgeable than most clergy in America," Jordan said, looking out into a crowd of what looked to be thousands of hostile Beautiful worshippers.

"But, I'll tell you what I do know. I know that my God, our God, is a just God. Our God is a fair God, and as I look out around our community I see prostitution, homelessness, drug dealing, poverty, and drunkenness. I see children being prepared by the streets to become thieves, murderers, and drug addicts." He pointed a finger in the air. "But, what I don't see is the church. Not Beautiful Baptist, but the black church, coming into the hoods and the schools and the courthouses and the hospitals and lobbying in DC to stop the destruction and desecration of our people and our communities."

"Whachu doin' about it?" an angry voice shouted from the first row.

Ignoring the man's outburst, he continued. "We get out and march when the Michael Bells draw media attention in towns like Jenna, Louisiana, but I been in prison, and I can tell you that there are hundreds of thousands of Michael Bells incarcerated in federal and state prisons all around America. And just like Michael Bell, they're victims of an unjust system," he struck a fist on the podium, "an ungodly system. And at 6:00, when the cameras are turned off, the marchers go home and our children are still left to rot in the catacombs of concrete and steel prison hells. As part of our protesting, we call ourselves crippling the economy by not buying gas or not spending money for one day, but what do we do the next day?" Jordan shook his head. "You know what we do. We spend twice as much money, buy even more gas or more of what we refused to buy the day of the protest. We support organizations like the NAACP, when they don't support us when it counts. Case in point: 1995, they ousted the largest positive movement by black men this nation has ever seen. And now, look what happened in the last presidential election. They supported a white woman running for president when we had a viable black candidate who, if he didn't do anything he'd promised, he would still do more than any white woman or man could do to the psyche of young black boys all around this country.

"Five and six year old boys will be saying I'm gon' be president, and instead of being behind a microphone practicing to be 50 cents, on a football field trying to be Terrell Owens, or shooting hoops in the park in hopes of being the next Kobe Bryant, they'll be behind books practicing to be President Barack Obama. We have to stop blaming others for our condition. It is us that let injustice persist in our community."

"You got that right," someone shouted from the congregation.

"Let me ask you all something?" He paused, his hands gripped the podium as he looked out at the faces of the community and the church. "Was Jesus a baller? Did He ride around in a gold chariot with twenty-six inch chrome rims? Was Jesus tailor-made from head to toe? Did Jesus have a big mansion on a hill?"

A few began to clap.

"Let me ask you something else? Through the hand of God, did Jesus not make a blind man see? He was such a great speaker that he talked Satan right up out of a young woman. So wouldn't you agree that it's fair to say, if Jesus wanted the riches of the world He would and could have achieved gold of an unimaginable measure? But instead, He lived among, and just as the common people had. They related to Him, they listened to Him, and He was able to create a revolution that has not been paralleled since His time. A revolution that is still going on, the God-fearing, seeing, unified revolution of love, truth, and equal justice. But to do this Jesus sacrificed His own life so we could be here."

"Amen! Amen! Amen!" a lady shouted.

"And we so scared and we so consumed by worldly things that we've reverted to a blind state, a dead state of being. I've got one last question. What are you," he waved an accusing finger around the church, "each and every one of you going to do now. Malcolm X said, put the word *freedom* out of you vocabulary if you're not willing to die for it. Are you ready?"

Jihad

Jordan smiled thinking of President Barack Obama's campaign slogan, *Yes We Can.* And we really can, if people are willing to sacrifice everything for change.

"Uncle Jordan?"

"Yes, princess?"

"What is a bitch?"

She caught him so off guard that he forgot he was in his pick-up headed home from church. He turned to his pretty little dolled-up niece. "Where did you hear that word, princess?"

A car horn blared.

He looked up just in time, cutting the wheel hard and speeding up, barely avoiding a collision with a black Hummer. He placed a hand over his heart. "Princess, I'm so sorry."

"Do it again! Do it again, Uncle Jordan," Ariel said as she bounced around in the child seat that he could never get her into correctly.

"I about had a heart attack and you're laughing like you just got off of a ride at Six Flags."

Her eyes got big. "Ooowee, you gon' take me and Weeble to Six Flags?"

Why did I have to mention Six Fags? Weak and unable to deny his precious three-year-old niece of most things, he said, "Not today, Princess, but," he smiled at her in the rear view mirror, "but soon I'll take you and Weeble to Six Flags."

"Weeble, you hear that?" She looked down at the teddy bear she held tightly in her arms. "Uncle Jordan is going to take us to Six Flags" she pointed a little finger at the pink

174

teddy bear. "That means you have to be good, or you won't go with me. Do you unn'erstand?"

A few minutes later, he pulled over to the curb in front of his home in the West End.

"You really promise to take us to Six Flags, Uncle Jordan?"

"Yes princess, I promise." He ran a finger through her long black hair.

"Cross your fingers, hope to die, stick a needle in your eye?" she asked.

"Cross my fingers, hope to die, stick ten needles in my eye," he said.

"Hope you ain't like Daddy," she said, looking down.

"What do you mean?"

"Daddy always promise stuff and he never does his promises."

He took off her seat belt. "Princess, has Uncle Jordan ever let you down?"

She shook her head.

He kissed her cheek. "And I never will."

"Uncle Jordan?"

"Yes, Princess."

"I asked mommy, but she told me I was too young to unn'erstand, but I'm a big girl, you know I am. I didn't even cry last time Daddy got mad and called Mommy bad names."

Jordan's eyes got big. "Yes, you are. You're Uncle Jordan's big girl."

She nodded her head in agreement before climbing out of the car. "If you tell me what that word means I promise I won't tell nobody," she shook her little head," that you told me."

He knelt down next to her and grabbed her little hands. "Where did you hear that word again, Princess?"

"Daddy. He calls Mommy bitch all the time. I know it's bad because he only says it when he's mad."

"He says the B word in front of you?"

She nodded her head up and down. "Sometimes, but mostly when they are arguing somewhere in the house where they think I can't hear them."

Jordan was so angry, he had to bite his tongue.

"Uncle Jordan?"

He ignored her. As he was still taking in what his niece had just said. He couldn't believe—No, yes, he could. Jevon treated all women the same. Even his wife, the woman Jordan loved. The woman Jordan never stopped loving. But how could he so blatantly disrespect his own child?

"Tickle, tickle, tickle," she said trying to tickle him under his arms.

"I'm sorry, Princess."

"You okay, Uncle Jordan?" A concerned look crossed her round almost four-year-old face.

"Yeah, I'm fine," he said.

She crossed her arms. "Okay, now back to my big girl question. Don't worry." She covered her Teddy bear's ears. "Weeble can't hear you. It's just us. We havin' a big-girl-big-uncle talk."

"Princess, a bitch is a female dog," he explained.

"Ohhhh, like a little puppy," she said as if she completely understood.

"Sorta kinda," he said, as he began walking up the sidewalk.

He hadn't taken but a couple of steps when he saw a shadow out the corner of his eye.

Chapter 31

"*U*h, hey, sugar, you got a square I can borrow?" a dolled-up little girl that had obviously come from the abandoned house next door asked. She couldn't have been older than fifteen, a baby.

"Nah, baby." He shook his head. "I don't smoke."

"You think you can loan me three dollars, then?" she asked sticking her little chest out.

It was warm outside but not that damn warm, he thought, as he looked at what she wore. She was a little bitty thing; no more than five-two, and that was with her black three-inch heels on. She had smooth butter-yellow skin. She wore a dusty, used-to-be-white mini-skirt so small that you could see her reddish-brown pubic hair. And a purple bra-like top supported her grapefruit-sized breasts. When she turned her head to the side, you could see that the new growth in her extensions was starting to cause her braids to unravel.

"I'm sorry, sweetie, I don't have any singles," he said, as he tried to hurry Ariel along.

"I can suck your dick for ten, or you can fuck me and I'll suck you off for twenty," she whispered as he tried to pass her.

He stopped and stared at her. "Ariel, sweetie, get back in the truck."

"Huh?" his niece asked. "I'm hungry."

"Just for a minute. I need to talk to this young lady. Pretend you're driving," he said, motioning toward the steering wheel. That seemed to satisfy her because she darted to the truck.

Jordan waited for her to get inside then he stepped closer to the girl. "How old are you?"

She licked her lips. "Old enough to suck, fuck, and make you nut," she said with confidence.

He reached into his back pocket and took out his wallet. "I tell you what," he waved his wallet in her direction, "tell me how old you are and I might let you take care of me."

"Seventeen."

"Okay." He nodded. "So, it's like that, huh?" Jordan said, turning around, and stepping back to the truck.

"It's like what?" she asked.

He turned his back toward her. "You playin' games, little girl." He shook his head. "I don't play games."

"Ain't nobody playin' no games."

"Telling me you seventeen is playing games. You know you ain't even close to being seventeen. I don't care how old you are." Slipping into street vernacular, he continued, "I ain't the po-po. I don't carry a badge. You ain't gotta fake the funk with me, Shawty."

"I'm fourteen, okay?" She put her hands on her little curvy hips. "So, can I take care of you now?"

He shook his head.

"We can go right in there," she said, pointing to the abandoned house next door.

"Does your mother know what you doin'?" Jordan asked.

"Uh, yeah," the girl said, her voice laced with sarcasm.

"I bet she does."

"Come on up, she's in the house. What? You wanna do me and my momma? That'll be forty, but for you... we'll do you for thirty. I bet you ain't never had a threesome with a mother and daughter."

And I never will, he thought. How could a mother turn her own teenage daughter out?

He looked at the concrete-chipped stairs leading to the house next door where she and her mother were tricking out of. They were covered with knee-high weeds, but he could still see the two clear blue crack sacks between the first and second stairs. He knew they were new because he'd just swept the ones up from last night this morning, before he and Ariel left for church.

At this point, he was at a loss for words. Ariel was probably burning up in the truck. He pulled a twenty out of his wallet. "I don't want your body. I want your mind. Here." He handed her the twenty. "Now go clean yourself up and get some food in your system."

"Thank you, uuh..."

"Jordan. The name's Jordan Hayes," he said to her back. "Oh, and I'll be watching you," he shouted, making a mental note to call children and family services after he dropped Ariel off.

Thoughts of Jevon clouded Jordan's head. His anger had simmered, but not by much.

Jordan held Ariel's little hand while they walked up the two sets of stairs leading to the front door of his house.

Jevon had tricked Jordan into buying a crack house that was in desperate need of repair. Jordan was fool enough to believe Jevon's story about the Atlanta University Center being in the process of buying up the land on his street and the next two streets over. He said they were going to fix up the abandoned houses and turn the others into boarding houses for students. Jordan believed him because the University was right up the street and they had already started building apartment-like student housing on the other side of Spelman and Morehouse College.

It wasn't until a few days ago that he'd made some calls and found out that there wasn't, and had never been, any plans to buy up the area where he lived.

Half of the houses on his street were abandoned crack houses. And before he got the loan to buy it, the house he now owned was the largest crack house on the street. It was a yellow five-bedroom Victorian manor, built in 1930. The only reason Jordan hadn't knocked his brother's teeth out was because after Jordan started the home rehabilitation process, he fell in love with the house, and the history of the neighborhood. The few people that did live on Jordan's block had been there at least two generations. The rich history of Drummond Street, as told by its inhabitants, made Jordan feel obligated to try and clean up the street. Afterward, his goal was to expand his efforts throughout the entire West End community.

For the third time today Jordan had let his mind linger, forgetting about his niece who was sitting at the small kitchen table coloring. "Princess, why are you coloring in that book? Is that a school book?" he asked, peering closer.

Without looking up, she said, "Nobody in it looks like me. In all my Little Bill books, the kids inside look like me and the kids at my school."

"Little girl, you are a trip," he said finishing up the pancakes, and turkey bacon he was cooking.

"I'm a big girl, and I am a vacation," she shouted.

"Huh?"

Still holding the brown crayon in her little hand, she said, "You called me little girl. I'm a big girl. You call me a trip. I'm a vacation."

He just smiled while preparing their plates.

She looked up. "Uncle Jordan?"

"Yes, Princess."

"Was that girl you were talking to when we was outside, was she a bitch?"

Oh Lord, what I have I started? No, what has Jevon started? He took the pot holder glove off. After placing the food on the table, he sat down across from his niece.

She got up and carried her plate to where he sat. After moving his plate to the side and putting hers down in front of him, she climbed up into his lap.

"Girl, you getting too big to be up in your uncle's lap."

"Them big ole muscles you got, I'll never be too big."

"In response to your last question, Princess, no, baby. That young girl I was talking to is a princess in disguise." Jordan pinched Ariel's cheeks and smiled. "She's just like you. Now, close your eyes and let's bless the food."

After they finished eating and cleaning up the dishes, he hurried Ariel out to the truck. *When I finish with Jevon he won't be putting his hands on any woman, ever again,* Jordan said to himself while getting Ariel situated in the car seat. While closing the truck's passenger-side door, he slipped. In hopes of breaking his fall, he reached out and grabbed the mailbox, which crashed to the sidewalk right beside him, sending a week worth of mail scattering everywhere.

Between working with the kids at the boys club, the community outreach he was doing, and tiling his bathroom and kitchen floor, he'd forgotten to check his mail. Ariel laughed while he gathered the mail and walked up the stairs to his front door. He was going to drop the mail inside when he noticed a dark blue envelope. He studied it a second. It didn't have a sender's name or return address on it.

He opened the door, tossed all the mail except the blue envelope onto a table near the door and raced back to the truck.

"Is that a birthday card?" Ariel asked when she saw him pull the envelope out. "'Cause it looks like a birthday card envelope."

He turned the envelope around. "I don't know, but I doubt it. You know when my birthday is."

"Yeah. It's the same as Daddy's, April 8. Are you going to open it?" she asked.

"Later, after I get you home."

"Well, can I open it?"

"Go ahead," he said, handing her the envelope as he pulled away from the curb.

A minute later, he glanced over at her.

"Surrrr-Sur-p-ee..."

"Surprise."

"Sur-prise," she repeated.

Jordan glanced over and noticed that it was a very colorful card with the word 'surprise' running from top to bottom at an angle. "Sweetie, let Uncle Jordan read it."

"Unhhhhhh, I wanna read it," she whined.

"I'll let you read it, but let your Uncle Jordan read it first, okay, Princess?"

"Ooooooookay." She was reluctant to give it up, but

after she did he put the card under his leg and she sat there with her arms crossed and her lip stuck out.

A few minutes later they pulled up in Cheyenne and Jevon's horseshoe driveway. Jordan parked in front of the stained glass front double doors before pulling the card from under his leg.

His eyes got wide. "No, she didn't." He shook his head in disbelief. "No, she did not." He quickly read the card four or five times. "Please, Lord, tell me this is a sick joke."

<u>Chapter 32</u>

*J*s this some kind of sick joke? Cheyenne wondered as she stared at the Caller ID on her cell phone. The only Cheryl Sharell she knew was from a ward back at Georgia Regional where she used to work.

"Hello, this is Dr. Jamison. I'm returning a phone call," Cheyenne said, sitting in the first of three rows inside her home theatre room. She'd popped in the disc Jevon had given her and was waiting for the DVD to boot up.

"Doc. What's crackin'?"

"Cheryl?"

"I prefer Cherry, but, yeah, this me."

"How'd you get my cell phone number? How are you even calling me? Cheyenne asked, hoping she had not escaped again.

"That's right, you don't know what happened."

"What do you mean?"

"A few months after you left to go into private practice, I got a conditional release."

"Really?"

"Yeah. Bishop Wiley got me released into his custody."

184

"Did he give you my number?"

"Don't even worry about all that. Look, I ain't callin' to shoot the shit. I need to see you. It's important," she said.

"Uhm, I don't know. I'm kind of—"

"Look, Doc. You the only one at that place that ever showed me any kind of love, and for that I am grateful. You stood up for me and the other girls on A ward. So now that I'm in the free world, I can repay the favor."

"I was just doing my job. You don't owe me anything."

"Doc! Look, like I said, this ain't a social call."

The video began to play. Cheyenne gasped at what she saw on her 125-inch theater screen. Monica was her friend, her best friend. Why?

"Doc? You there? Doc?"

"I have to go. I have to go," Cheyenne said, hanging up.

A few minutes later, Cherry's face came into view on the screen. "What in God's name?" she said aloud as Cherry, Monica, and Jevon engaged in three-way oral sex.

Cheyenne redialed Cherry. "Where and when do you wanna meet?" she asked after Cherry picked up.

"How 'bout, in an hour at—"

"No, that's too soon. I have something to take care of. Will five o'clock work for you?" Cheyenne asked.

"You got somewhere in mind?" Cherry asked.

Cheyenne smiled. "Yep, I sure do. But let me call you back after I speak to an old friend. I'm sure she'll let us use her place. I just have to wait until she gets out of church. I'll call you back by three, to let you know for sure."

"Okay, but please call me back; it's a matter of life and death, literally," Cherry said, before ending the call.

Chapter 33

" *H*ow long?"

"How long what?" Monica asked, as soon as they were seated for the live jazz and Sunday brunch at Paschal's Restaurant, located right around the corner from where Jordan lived.

After taking a sip and placing the glass of lemonade down, Cheyenne reached inside her Coach bag and slammed the DVD on the table. "How long have you been fucking Jevon?"

"I'm... I don't know what to say?" Monica dropped her head in shame.

"Well, you damn sure knew what to say while you were making this, this pornographic video production."

"No, he didn't?"

"Yes he did," Cheyenne said. "Why, Monica? All the men in Georgia, why sleep with him?"

"I'm sorry."

"We were friends, best friends, or so I thought," Cheyenne said.

"You don't care about him. You haven't slept with the man since Jordan's been out, and that's, what, about six months now?"

"Monica, that isn't the point. You know everything this man has done to me. You know my pain. I could care less about me being married to him. I cannot believe..." Cheyenne broke down. "I loved you like a sister, all we've been through together."

Monica was crying now as well. "I don't know. I just, I just... I'm sorry. I just wanted to feel a man, any man, and I was so attracted to his physique and his looks. I know he was off limits. I know. I know," she cried.

"Ladies, are you two okay?" a middle-aged, salt-and-pepper-haired Nigerian-looking waiter asked.

Monica nodded as Cheyenne said, "We're fine, thank you." She took out a couple pieces of tissue and handed one to Monica.

"I love you, Chey, I swear I do. I never meant to... I didn't think..." She shook her head. "There's no excuse. Nothing I can say—"

"You're married to an older version of Jevon."

Monica nodded. "I know. I know. It was lust. After we were together the first time, a couple months back, we just kept at it. I despise him, Chey, I really do. It's just his dick and his tongue. I'm..."

"Monica!"

"I'm being honest," Monica said.

"I get the picture," Cheyenne said before switching gears and asking, "How do you know Cheryl?"

"Cheryl who?"

"Your co-star, on the DVD."

"Cherry?"

"Yes, Cherry."

"I don't really know her. Jevon introduced us. And how about she thinks Jevon is Jordan."

"Monica." Cheyenne reached for her friend's hand. After Monica placed her hand in Cheyenne's, Cheyenne continued. "Do you really love me? I mean, how do you really feel about me? Really?"

She looked into Cheyenne's watery eyes. "Outside of my cousin, Joanne, there is no one that I love more. Whether you ever talk to me or trust me again, I'll cherish you as my once real and best friend."

"I can't say when or if I'll ever fully trust you again, but I love you, too, and I need you, especially now," Cheyenne said.

"Ladies, will you be having the brunch today," the waiter asked, refilling their glasses.

The women looked at each other, and at the same time, they said, "No, thank you."

"Well, if you change your mind I'll be in this section," he said, waving his arm around the small area in the back of the restaurant where they were seated.

"Anything, girl." Monica squeezed Cheyenne's hand. "You name it, and I'll do anything to begin earning your trust."

*****

An hour later, Monica, and Cherry were sitting on a bicycle rack in front of the One Free Boy's Club, waiting for Cherry.

"How'd you get this place," Monica asked.

"My girl, Rhythm. You know, the one married to Moses King, head of the One Free family. I introduced you two at New Dimensions First Church of God, remember?"

Cheyenne said. "And who don't know about Moses and Rhythm One Free? They only the new millennium Malcolm X and Harriett Tubman."

"You right about that, girl," Monica said.

"Because of all the positive things they're doing through their One Free Nation, and the New Dimensions church, I've been doing a little volunteer work for them, screening ex-felons who apply for their church's College Freedom Fund Scholarship. Anyway, she's letting us use the Boy's Club."

"Oh, I get it now," Monica said.

"You get what?"

"That's how Jordan got the counseling job so fast after getting released from prison."

Monica and Cheyenne stood up at the same time as they saw Cherry walking down the sidewalk. With an air of diva-like confidence she stepped in long, determined strides. Cherry had on dark glasses. Her hair was pulled back into a pony tail. The sun seemed to shine on the woman wearing all red.

"What is she doing here?" Cherry asked.

"Let's go inside," Cheyenne said, leading the way through the club's glass doors. "I'll explain everything, and, I have lots of questions for you, Cheryl."

"Uhm-Uhm, I bet you do," she said, looking at Monica, before turning her attention back toward Cheyenne. "And I got lots of answers. Maybe not the ones you wanna hear, but trust and believe girl, I got answers." Cherry followed Cheyenne and Monica inside the large building.

Chapter 34

*J*t had been a week and their plan was in motion. It had taken everything in Monica's power to act natural. But that's just what she was doing as she and her husband piled into his Rolls.

"I can't wait to hear what type of silly answers you come up with," Bishop Wiley said as he pulled the Rolls out of one of six garages connected to his massive estate home.

"You talkin' to me?" Monica asked.

"No, I'm talking to the dashboard."

"Smartass, you could've been on the phone."

He pushed the stereo system's play button located on the steering wheel.

Monica smiled as she looked out of the passenger's window. There was nothing CW could say that would ruin her good mood. Today was the big day.

"Who's pussy is this? Huh. Talk to me," Jevon's voice floated out of the sixteen speaker stereo system.

Monica's head jerked around.

"It's, oh shit, daddy, this pussy got your name on it."

190

She stared at the small screen on the Rolls' dashboard.

"I'm gonna be free, oh yeahhhh," CW sang, his version of the Ohio Player's old school hit.

"I don't know why you singin' and smilin'."

"Isn't a beautiful day. I mean, the sun is shining. I'm mega rich and I'm about to get rid of a disease I've had for three years, five months and twenty-two days. That's why I'm singing and smiling." He nodded. "I'm pretty excited, Broomhilda."

"Me too, mini-man," Monica said. "I get so wet just thinking about a real man's dick up in me." She put a hand up her dress. "Will you look at that stroke? Look at that big brown dick up in me," she said, referring to the video playing on the Rolls' DVD player. "Doesn't that just excite you?"

"No, it doesn't, but this does." He pointed to the ten-inch screen on the dashboard. "This is my favorite part," he said as Monica put a leg over Cherry's face while Jevon put his penis in Monica's mouth.

"You are really into this shit. Looking at a grown man's dick excites you. I bet your little teeny, tiny, beanie weenie is hard."

"It wasn't so tiny when it was halfway down your throat, now was it?" He smiled. "Deep throat."

"Uhm, you must have me confused with one of your boyfriends." She licked the finger that was up her dress a second ago. "Come to think of it, I wouldn't be surprised if Jevon fucked you in the ass, or maybe he stopped that big mouth of yours up with his man-sized dick."

The video still played on the Rolls' DVD player as they spoke. Monica fought to hold back a moan as she continued watching Jevon slide in and out of her. She had to cross her legs to prevent herself from having an orgasm.

"We'll see who fucks who when the judge doesn't give you nothing but a hard way to go. Can you say half? Half of nothing." He laughed.

If he only knew. Monica didn't want to play her hand. She had entirely too much to do once she got inside the church.

"You better enjoy your last Sunday walking the red mile," the bishop said, knowing how much Monica loved strutting her stuff down the long red carpeted middle aisle toward the concert-like stage. "You think I should cry when I give the bishops' wives a copy of the DVD? Or should I just look like a sick puppy?" he asked, sticking his bottom lip out and batting his eyes.

"Don't think this is over." She smiled. "Please believe, I have something very special in store for you, Bishop Clarence Wendell Wiley."

"What? Crabs, VD, Herpes, AIDS?" he said, laughing. "No, that can't be, because I haven't been up in that sewer hole of yours in such a long while."

"Keep laughin', you arrogant son of a bitch." She pointed a finger at him as they passed the ATM and tithing booth at the entrance to the huge Beautiful Baptist megaplex. "You know dickless wonder, I would talk about your momma, but she's dead, and someone once told me if you don't have anything nice to say about the dead, don't say anything at all." She looked up at CW and smiled. "Your momma's dead, good."

"And like a carton of spoiled milk, your mother and father threw you away at birth. And all it took was me smiling at your foster mother and I took what was left of your innocence at such a young age." He placed a hand over his heart. "Oh, that teenage tight virgin twat, was so, so good. I just regret that I can't rip you apart again.

Remember the anguish, the screams, and your unanswered cries?"

Tears started to well up in her eyes. *No, Monica. No, don't cry. Don't let him get to you. You have too much to do. Very soon he'll get his. Just stay focused.*

"Ahhhh, no comeback. Surely, you have more to say, after all, you wasted most of your life trying to get back at me for jamming my horse dick up in you," he said. "Am I turning you on, Witchie Poo?"

She took a deep breath. She dabbed her eyes with a Kleenex, right before getting out of the bishop's new purple and gold, Phantom Rolls Royce. *Play your role girl. Smile. Don't let him or the church see you in a frazzled state.* She took a deep breath and used her hands to smooth out her eight-hundred-dollar Versace loose-fitting platinum belted white dress, matching open-toe white heels, and a string of white pearls. The pearl-beaded tiara she wore helped keep her hair pinned back in place.

Bishop Wiley and his wife walked together hand in hand, making their way up the stairs and into the church vestibule as if they were the happiest couple in the world.

Once inside, Monica said, "I'll be back in a minute." She turned and walked away before CW could get a word out in protest.

After locking the restroom door behind her, she took the infrared scope out of her purse, slipped her heels off and climbed on top of the toilet seat. She had to put the scope in her mouth while moving the ceiling tile off of its track. Afterward, she ran a hand on the inside of the opening until she felt the assault rifle she'd put in place Wednesday evening after bible study. When she felt the warm steel, she took the scope out of her mouth and placed it beside the gun's stock. Satisfied that she'd done her part, she replaced the tile and got down from the toilet.

Chapter 35

*O*nce Bishop and Monica Wiley ascended the stage, the shooter walked through the church's vestibule sliding doors, along with a large group of other members and visitors, all waiting to be ushered up into the balcony to hear the Word of God as only the Bishop C. Wendell Wiley could deliver.

Although nervous, the shooter paid attention to everything and everyone. She knew how to use a gun, but she had never used one to kill another human being. But, with the help of the Internet and her Playstation 3, she was confident that she'd hit her target.

The first thing the shooter noticed was the blinking red lights on the smoke detectors. "Damn," she muttered. The unobtrusive smoke-detector-like cameras were on the walls all over the vestibule. Nervous, she did her best to scan the large open area, looking for anyone that seemed out of place.

She had to think fast. There was no way she was going back to that place and she knew Monica would crack under pressure if the law got a hold of her. There was no telling how long the cameras had been there. Who knows, there might be cameras in the women's restroom. Even if there weren't, who's to say that the cameras in the vestibule didn't pick up any part of the gun or the scope when Monica brought them through the entrance?

As Cherry made her way to the women's restroom, she had no doubt that if the cops put the pressure on, Monica would crack like an egg. Monica really didn't know Cherry. She had no allegiance to her, so why not tell the cops whom she paid to carry out the hit? The only person who really knew Cherry, was Cheyenne, and after all she'd done for her, there was no way Cherry would let anything happen to her. And as much shit as Monica was into, Cherry had no doubt that Monica would take any and everybody down to save her own ass.

"Excuse me, Excuse me," Cherry said, squeezing through the crowd as ushers began directing people up the escalators and to the balcony aisles where seating was available.

Once inside the restroom, Cherry went to the sink and pretended to study herself in the mirror as if her make-up was askew, or a hair was out of place.

"Good morning, sister," a heavyset woman said without looking up as she stood at one of several fancy glass sinks washing her hands.

"Good morning to you," Cherry replied.

"You ladies better hurry up; you don't wanna miss the drawing," a middle-aged graying version of Toni Braxton said after leaving the toilet stall that Cherry needed to get into.

"I almost forgot. This is the third Sunday," the heavyset woman said, wiping her hands on her pants, before rushing to the door.

"What drawing?" Cherry asked.

"You must be a first-time visitor," the older lady said, as she, too, washed her hands.

"Yes, ma'am." Cherry nodded. "I am."

"This is the third month that Bishop Wiley has drawn a registered tithing member's name out of a box."

"Registered tithing member?"

"Yeah, you know members who have their W-2's on file and are current with their tithes."

What a scam artist, Cherry thought.

"What's that look on your face, and why're you shaking your head, young lady?"

"No reason, just thinking."

"I hope you're not trying to judge," the middle-aged lady said.

"I'm sorry," Cherry said.

"I said," the lady put a hand on her hips, "I hope you aren't insinuating anything."

"Ma'am, I don't have the slightest idea what you're talking about," Cherry said.

"You shook your head right after I told you that the Bishop drew a name from a box with only Beautiful Baptist registered tithing member's names."

"Why would I—"

"Sista girl," the short, graying, petite woman interrupted, "let me tell you something. Bishop is the best thing that has ever happened to black people. Look what he's doing for the community. He tore down them raggedy, hood rat projects in Conyers and built that new Christian shopping mall, and him and Bishop TJ Money done gone into drug infested communities all over the city and tore down project housing and built Christian custom homes. And on top of that he's even given some of his homes away to the less fortunate, and for the last three months on third Sunday, Bishop has given away a five thousand dollar gift certificate, good for any store in his new luxurious Conyers Center City Mall. I get so tired of you sinners judging saints," the woman said, while opening the bathroom door.

Without turning and saying goodbye, the woman continued. "He's even sponsoring a jazz concert in the Beautiful Baptist amphitheater this Friday coming, and ten of each fifty-dollar admission fee will go to the Beautiful Baptist Youth College Fund."

And they say I'm nuts, Cherry thought as the lady did her damndest to slam the bathroom door.

After looking around the restroom and making sure there were no hidden cameras, she looked up at the return vent on the wall to her left, before taking out and unfolding a copy of the church's blueprints.

The plan had been for her to grab the gun, attach the scope and crawl about thirty feet down the shaft until she came out at the west end of the church, right under the projector room. There she'd be able to get off a clear shot. But now, things had changed. She knew those smoke detector cameras oh so well. She was the one that turned CW on to them in the first place. They were the same ones used to make the movie four months ago at the hotel. *And that dumb ass Jordan thought I didn't know.*

The twenty-five-thousand-dollar deposit that Monica had already given Cherry to kill her husband was appreciated. Although she would've taken the bishop out for free if Monica couldn't have paid. Everything Monica had told her about what the bishop had done to her, was just that much more motivation for Cherry to do what she'd already planned before she was released from the institution.

But now things had gotten complicated. If she would've known Dr. Jamison and Monica were so close, she wouldn't have struck the deal with CW to befriend his wife and frame her.

She now had the assault rifle and was screwing on the scope before she realized she hadn't locked the bathroom door. Quickly, she ran over and turned the lock.

"Is someone in there," a hand banged on the door, not two seconds after she'd locked it.

Ignoring the lady's voice, Cherry climbed on top of the sink and studied the blueprint one more time before folding it up and putting it back into her pocket.

"The door's locked. I don't know..." Cherry heard someone say outside the bathroom door.

She didn't waste time in unscrewing the four screws that held the large return vent in place.

"Hey, is someone in there?" a male voice asked while banging on the door.

After quietly sliding the rifle through the vent, she hoisted herself up and climbed through. A minute later she'd managed to spread some type of glue on the vent and stuck it back in place.

As she awkwardly scooted through the heating and air metal box-like maze with the rifle between her legs, she thought of how so many men had played her and had played other women that had crossed her path, but Bishop Wiley was the worst of the worst. People like him are bigger than the law. People like him had to be dealt with by other means. She smiled as she crawled around a corner. After twenty minutes of knee, hip and elbow-bruising maneuvering, she finally saw light. A few moments later she was at her new destination.

She peeked out of the vent, satisfied that the coast was clear, she kicked the vent a couple times, knocking the screws out. The third kick sent the eighteen-inch return vent crashing to the floor. Although no one should have been in the basement, Cherry was relieved that sheets, table cloths, and choir robes muffled the noise that the metal vent should have made. With the AK clutched to her chest, she slid out and dropped onto the dirty tablecloths and choir robes, before rising to her knees and scanning the dark room. The only things in it were three washing machines, three dryers, a couple of picnic tables, a few chairs, two sinks, and several irons and ironing boards.

Before leaving the room, she wiped the scope and the gun clean before placing them in the middle of a mountain of dirty laundry.

Chapter 36

"*Y*ou what?" Monica shouted.

"I left the AK in the church laundry room under a pile of robes and tablecloths," Cherry said, standing outside of her old school red Hyundai Excel, in the back of a Kroger grocery store parking lot, not too far from the forty-two acre Beautiful Baptist megaplex.

Monica leaned against her platinum-colored Lincoln Navigator, smoking a Newport. "You have to be abso-fucking-lutely kidding me, right? I mean, tell me you didn't do no dumb shit like that. Got damn!" she said, turning and kicking her front tire.

"The tire don't kick back, sweetie," Cherry said.

"What the fuck you say to me?"

"I said," she spoke louder, "the tire don't kick back."

"Bitch, you think 'cause you did a few years in a loony bin, I'm supposed to be scared?" Monica said, taking a step toward Cherry.

"I don't think shit," Cherry calmly said. "But I do know that if you call me one more bitch, I'm gon' break my foot off in yo ass, and I don't wanna do that. I just had my toes done yesterday."

"Hold on." Monica took another step forward. "Just hold the fuck on."

"I already told you that he had the same type of surveillance system installed in and around the church that he had at the *W* hotel that night. I know because I'm the one that told him about the manufacturer."

"So why am I not in jail?" Monica asked, her arms crossed and her feet tapping on the gravelly pavement.

"Because you probably had enough intelligence to completely conceal the rifle when you took it into the restroom Wednesday evening."

"So, you mean to tell me, his freaky, perverted ass didn't have no cameras in the women's restroom?"

"Obviously not," Cherry said.

"So, why'n the hell didn't you go through with the plan?" Monica asked while banging a fist onto the Navigator's hood.

Cherry shook her head, thinking that this bitch needed some serious help. "Okay, the police would've took the tapes and saw me going into the restroom and never coming out. I would've been in jail before sundown."

"Shit, we still goin' to jail. You left an illegal assault rifle and an infrared scope behind."

"Sweetie, first, you might wanna take some of that fire out of your voice. Second, we ain't goin' to nobody's jail. I wiped the prints off. Trust and believe, I ain't gon' be locked up ever again."

"So how we gon' get the gun out the laundry room?"

"What is it with this *we* shit?" Cherry pointed a finger at Monica. "Look, sister, I ain't gon' lie, I need the money, but I didn't agree to do this shit for the money. I'm doing this because that mothafucka you married is the worst kind of evil, an evil that spreads like a lethal virus. A virus that is immune to reason, or the United States injustice system."

Monica interrupted. "So, I guess you're the cure."

"No, sweetie. I'm just a woman that specializes in the handling of piece-of-shit men. And your husband is the worst of the worst. Trust and believe, the Bishop C. Wendell Wiley's demise is near. As soon as I take care of some unfinished business with Mr. Hayes," Cherry smiled, "Mr. Wiley will be next, I promise."

"What's your obsession with Jevon?" Monica asked.

"Who's Jevon?"

Monica shook her head, remembering that Cherry thought Jevon was Jordan. "I meant Jordan." Monica didn't really know why she didn't tell Cherry that Jevon wasn't Jordan. Maybe because she admired the man Jordan had become. Although she didn't know what Cherry was planning to do to Jordan, she knew that he had been through enough, and if anything bad happened to any man it might as well be Jevon. Especially after everything he had done to Chey.

"Well, since we are sort of blood sisters, I guess I can tell you. About seven years ago, Jordan was smokin' like a locomotive. He was my boo, and I made sure he was never without crack or pussy. All he did was smoke crack, eat pussy, and fuck. Anyway, he let two bitches whip my ass and put this scar on my face while he sat in a corner smoking that shit. The same shit I went out and robbed a nigga for. So, anyway, next thing I know, I'm wakin' up with restraints on and bright-ass lights in my face."

"You were in the hospital?" Monica said as more of a question than a statement.

"I wish it was just a hospital. Sweetie, I woke up scarred, swollen, and bandaged in the maximum security Georgia Regional mental institution hospital."

"Why were you there?"

"That's a long story, but the short version is that I had escaped from two medium security institutions in the past. And I'm not going to go into why I was there in the first place. Let's just say, every man that has ever fucked me," she smiled, "I've always come back to fuck them harder."

"Okay, I can't say I know what you mean. I don't even know if I wanna know, but what I do wanna know is how we," she shook her head, "I mean, how and when are you going to kill my husband."

"I don't have the slightest idea."

"What do you—"

She stuck a finger in the air. "Not now I don't, but give me a day or two. By then, I'll know the how and when. But as for the here and now, you need to get back to that church and get that rifle."

"I can do that, but in the meantime can we please continue to keep this between you and me. I love Cheyenne to death, but I can't just tell her that I'm about to kill CW. You don't know her like I do. She will flip."

"Sweetie, you don't know the Doc like I do. You'd be surprised what she knows and what she can handle, but I'll respect your wishes," Cherry said. "After you get out with the gun, I want you to text me the numbers 1,2,3,4. If you see anything that doesn't look right, walk away," Cherry said before turning and getting into her car.

Monica got back inside her custom SUV. "Shit.! Shit! Shit!" she said, banging both fists on the steering wheel. A minute later, she started the vehicle. Cherry had said a day or two. That was a day or two too late as far as Monica was concerned. There was no telling what CW would do or when he'd do it, she thought while driving. *Fuck it. I've come too far to turn back now. I came into this world by myself and I'll leave this bitch by myself. I don't need anyone to fight my battles. Cherry was right, the man was a disease, a virus.* No, she shook her head. *I won't give him the satisfaction of taking me down. He will not make a fool of me in front of his precious congregation.*

She passed through the twenty-foot-high wrought iron gates leading into the Beautiful Baptist church megaplex. Her eyes teared up as she thought about all the lives that have been lost because of CW. All the years she'd spent trying to ruin him, and now it had come to this. He'd be dead, but he'd die a hero to the black community. Life just wasn't fair, she thought while pulling into the covered parking space, reserved for the First Lady.

Still, he had to die right now. With tears of rage running down her face, ruining her make-up, she was determined to do what Cherry hadn't. She cut the engine, took off her seat belt and was about to open the door when Whodini's old school hit, *Friends* began playing. She smiled, remembering Cheyenne downloading the ringtone to both of their phones so they'd know when one called the other.

Chapter 37

"*D*on't do it," Cheyenne said, as soon as Monica picked up.

"Don't do what?"

"Whatever you're thinking about doing?"

"I don't know what you're talking about, Chey," Monica said into the phone.

"Look, girl, I just got off the phone with Cheryl." Before Monica could protest, Cheyenne continued. "She didn't tell me what was going on. She just told me she'd just left you and that she thought you were about to do something crazy."

"Girl, you know me. I always think before I act. Besides," she sniffed, "Cherry don't know me. Who she think she is?"

"Girl, are you crying," Cheyenne interrupted.

"What gives her the right to call you and say," she sniffed, "that I was about to do something crazy?"

"She's an authority on crazy. Monica, I don't know how much you know about Cheryl, or how deep you're really involved with her. Maybe I should have told you after the three of us met at the Boy's Club, but I didn't because technically she is—was a patient of mine."

"What are you talking about, Chey?" Monica asked while putting her leg back inside the SUV and closing the door.

Monica heard her friend let out a loud sigh on the other end of the phone.

"I don't have to tell you how much trouble I'll be in if anyone finds out that I violated a doctor-patient confidentiality."

"Girl, this is me. You know I would never say or do anything that..." Monica paused, thinking that she had fucked this woman's husband, and even after all the foul things he'd done to Cheyenne, and to herself, she still craved his manhood.

"I know you wouldn't," Cheyenne said, surprising Monica.

"Girl, I really am sorry about..."

"I know you are, girl. Jevon is so yesterday," she said, reading over last month's bank statement—the one that reflected a thirteen hundred dollar rental payment to an upscale apartment complex — one she didn't have a clue about. "Come on, we're past that now, right?"

"Girl," she paused, thinking that instead of sitting in the church parking lot talking to Cheyenne, she really wanted Jevon's manhood inside her mouth. "After that negro made that little home movie of me with my ass in the air, I wish I would fuck with him again. Cheyenne, you just don't know how much I want to do something to that man for putting me on—"

"Girl, don't worry about Jevon. He'll get his. I can promise you that," Cheyenne said into the Bluetooth earpiece while loading the nickel plated .38.

"Okay, now what's the story with your girl, Cherry?" Monica asked.

"Less than ten minutes after she was born, her father slit her mother's throat?"

"Nooo," Monica replied.

"It was either that or, let Cherry tell it, the CIA was going to kill him, Cheryl, and her mother."

"The CIA?"

"That's what Cheryl says. Let her tell it, her father, Charles Sharell, was a contract killer solely for the CIA, at least that was until he started freelancing in the mid 70's and early 80's."

"The Surgeon, Daddy Cool's son, was Cherry's father?" Monica asked.

"You know about him?"

"Girl, you know I read all the street novels. Daddy Cool was a legend, and he was real. He was rumored to have never shot a man. He nor his son."

"So, I've heard," Cheyenne said.

"I can't believe she is the granddaughter of Cool. Hell, her father was ice water himself — they say, he was so cool, he didn't sweat. Legend, has it that the Surgeon, was so bad that he could burn water and kill concrete."

Cheyenne laughed. "You really are fascinated by this."

"You're not?"

"I don't necessarily believe everything I heard about her father or grandfather. It's too fantastic," Cheyenne said.

"The name, Daddy Cool, fit his father's MO, but it never fit the son's. It was not long after establishing a name for himself among the underworld and top political official circles, when people started calling him the Surgeon. They say the man was as precise and accurate as a brain surgeon when it came to carrying out a hit."

"And the fact that he always used a scalpel on his victims probably helped in him being called the Surgeon," Cheyenne said.

"I read the part about Daddy Cool and his son, the Surgeon, never firing a gun, but I never read anywhere about the Surgeon, being a contract killer for the CIA. The book *Son of Cool* definitely didn't mention any of that," Monica said.

"That CIA part of the story is suspect. I did some research when Cherry first told me the story, and to this day I have never found any evidence that remotely links her father to the CIA. But, I did find it odd that a black man living in the 70's and early 80's tied to the murder and disappearance of almost a dozen prominent and politically connected white men had never spent a night behind bars."

Monica interrupted. "And don't forget, he was able to go into Chicago's Good Samaritan Hospital, slit his baby mother's throat and take his newborn daughter out of the hospital undetected."

"Damn, girl, you know all about the infamous Charles Sharell," Cheyenne said.

"Me and every black man and woman who's been to prison. Charles Sharell's biography, *Son of Cool* as told by the authors Jamise and Jihad, is as popular as any Donald Goines book."

"Yeah, that may be so, but somebody needs to write Cherry's story. Her mother was the black Marilyn Monroe, and she was often seen with America's most prominent movers and shakers back then."

"I know," Monica interrupted. "She was fucking some married politician tied to the Russian mob. Apparently the hit was placed on Cherry's mother because she must've overheard or saw something she wasn't supposed to."

"That's what the book states, but Cheryl told me that it had nothing to do with the Russian mob. She seems to think that the politician her mother was messing with at the time was not only being groomed for the presidency, but had strong ties to the mob. She tried to blackmail him, so the CIA called on the Surgeon to eliminate her," Cheyenne said.

"I don't get it. If Cherry's father got orders to hit her mother, then how did..."

"Okay, now this is where the story gets really convoluted," Cheyenne said. "Cheryl told me that late one evening her father entered her mother's apartment bedroom. Mind you, this all happened before Cheryl was even thought of. Anyway, Cherry's father had every intention of slitting Cheryl's mothers throat, and he would have if she didn't have a gun pointed at him. For an hour, they spoke in the dark. Cherry's mother explained that she was a contract killer who'd been given the opportunity to live if she killed the Surgeon."

"You got to be kidding," Monica said.

"Girl, I am dead serious."

"So what about the black Marilyn Monroe persona?" Monica asked.

"It was an image the CIA, her employer, had created and built up over the years. Her job was to try and get close to state representatives, senators, governors, and presidents."

"Hold on, Chey. You mean to tell me she worked for the CIA, too, come on now."

"Hey, I'm just telling you what I was told. Anyway, Cherry told me that her mother was hired to kill her father, because he'd compromised the CIA by becoming a freelance killer."

"So why didn't Cherry's mother kill the Surgeon?" Monica asked.

"Because after they spoke they came to the conclusion that after one killed the other, the CIA would just have the surviving hitter killed or framed for the dead killer's murder."

"Damn, this shit is better than fiction," Monica said.

"Girl, you haven't heard the half of it." Cheyenne said. "How about the two of them staged a shootout in the kitchen of the apartment Cheryl's mother rented. And Cherry told me that a bullet hit an open gas line causing the apartment to explode. Before the coroner pronounced dead the unidentifiable charred remains of the male and female found in the apartment, Charles and Cherry's mother were on their way from DC to Chicago."

"So, what, the two of them fell in love?" Monica asked.

"No, they decided to stick together for a while until they figured out what to do. And, who knows, "Cheyenne shrugged, "They just started having sex."

"Wow," Monica said.

Cheyenne continued. "It had been a little over a year since the two of them were pronounced dead in the New York apartment fire. Cherry's mother had never been pregnant. She'd also never missed taking a birth control pill in over ten years. That's why she ignored the signs and didn't realize she was pregnant until she was four months gone."

"Okay, okay. Girl, get to the point. What happened?"

"I forget exactly what Cherry said, but somehow the CIA tracked them down. While Cherry's mother was in labor at *Good Samaritan*, the agency contacted Charles and told him that he either walk into the hospital delivery room and kill her or they would kill him, her, and the baby. So, having no choice and no time to think, he walked in and slit the mother's throat, causing a big enough distraction for him to get away with baby Cheryl bundled in his arms."

"Damn! So where'd they go?" Monica asked.

"All over. They never stayed in one place for too long. By the time she was six, Cheryl could hit the bulls eye on a dart board from teen feet away. By the age of twelve, she was hitting the bulls eye from twenty feet away with a pair of dark shades covering her eyes. She became an expert with knives, scalpels and darts. She knew every muscle, bone, pressure point, and kill point in the human body."

"What did they do for money?" Monica asked, thinking that this story was totally different and even better than the book.

"I never said Charles didn't have money. He had lots of it. The man lived a frugal lifestyle. Instead of spending it, he put most of it in bank safe deposit boxes all over the Midwest. So, for years they had lived well off the money he'd earned carrying out government-sanctioned and unsanctioned hits. But, by the time Cheryl turned fifteen, they only had enough money to get through another six months. So father and daughter decided to do a job together. Instead of being hired to hit someone, Charles, decided to rob and hit a drug kingpin. The hit was to be the first for father and daughter. The victim was a kingpin crack-cocaine dealer named Elmo Black."

"Elmo Black. Elmo Black," Monica repeated. "Where have I heard that name?"

"Elmo was especially chosen because it was a known fact that he was into young girls. Charles had trained his daughter well; he had no worries on sending a fifteen-year-old child into the drug kingpin's lair."

Monica interrupted. "How could he get his own teenage daughter mixed up with a child-molesting drug dealer?"

"Monica, Cheryl was not your typical, ponytail-wearing teenage girl. She'd been homeschooled by her father for thirteen years. At the age of three he had her reading on a first grade level. By the time she was ten, she was reading Marx, Mao, and Sun Tzu—for fun. Anyway, Cheryl was inside the kingpin's well-guarded home, in Miami, for three days. In that time, she witnessed Elmo and his underlings drug the young girls and pass them around like bags of popcorn."

"How'd she avoid the same fate?" Monica asked.

"She didn't." The drug dealer and his cronies shot her up with heroine and raped her repeatedly. When she didn't call her father at the appointed time, he panicked. The only thing he could think of was his baby girl. By the time he killed the two men that stood guard outside the security gates and the two men that stood guard in the driveway, the drug kingpin had gathered the six men in the house and they lay in wait for him.

"Charles had untied his daughter and was carrying her naked body out of a bedroom when the kingpin and his henchmen ambushed him. Charles managed to kill two of the men before someone hit him in the head with a baseball bat."

"Shit!" Monica shouted.

"Charles woke up to his daughter's screams. A minute later, tied to a chair, a couple feet from the king-sized bed his daughter lay on, Charles's legs began to spasm right before he went into cardiac arrest while watching his daughter being ravaged by the men."

"In *The Son of Cool*, Jamise and Jihad stated that the Surgeon killed the seven armed men, with a surgeon's scalpel."

"Now that isn't quite true," Cheyenne said. "Cheryl told me that her father slipped her a scalpel before taking her into his arms."

"Okay, you mean to tell me a fifteen-year-old girl, who'd just been drugged and gang raped, fought off seven men?" Monica asked. "You couldn't write this in a book. No one would believe it."

"I'm just telling you the story as it was told to me," Cheyenne said. "All the men were found dead with their dick's in their mouths. And although Cheryl was never formally charged with the murders, she was charged with conspiracy to commit murder and perjury. After failing her psychiatric evaluation, it was ordered that she not stand trial, but be admitted to a mental institution for an indefinite period of time. Two years later, she escaped for the first time."

"Get outta here. That woman is off the chain," Monica said.

"Oh, yes, she was and still is," Cheyenne said. "She managed to elude authorities for three years, until Crazy Craig Sommers."

"Who?"

"Craig Sommers. He was a sadistic pimp that branded a C on the vaginas of the women in his stable."

"There are some sick bastards out there," Monica said.

"I know. I'm the one who's charged with delving into their minds."

"Okay, so what happened with this Craig cat?"

"Cheryl castrated the man, right before the police arrived. Sliced his penis off right inside the man's own living room, with three of his girls watching. This time she wasn't charged with anything."

"Are you serious?"

"Yep. Each of the three women that saw what happened gave statements saying that they castrated Craig. Although she wasn't charged — no one was — Cheryl was again sent back to the Milledgeville Mental Institution."

"Damn," Monica said, thinking that she almost got into it with a woman crazier than she was.

"And the next time she escaped, she killed four men, three known drug dealers and one part-time pimp. And all of them were found dead, with their penis's surgically removed, sticking out of their mouths."

"Let me guess, she wasn't charged with anything, right?" Monica said.

"That's right. No one saw or heard anything, and there was no DNA evidence or fingerprints that linked her to any of these men."

"So, how do you know she had anything to do with them?" Monica asked.

"Because after she was caught the last time, she was transferred to the maximum-security unit at Georgia Regional, where I worked. Cheryl, was on my caseload. It took a couple years, but she began to trust and open up to me. She told me how and why she did the others."

"How did she manage to keep escaping?"

"She never told me that, but she never escaped again after they sent her to Georgia Regional."

"How long was she there?"

"Close to five years."

"What made the state let that crazy bitch out after only serving five years?" Monica asked.

"You know how," Cheyenne said.

"Yeah, but how the hell would they even let her out under CW's care."

"Your guess is as good as mine," Cheyenne said.

"CW can't know that girl's history?"

No one does. *No one but me and you,* Cheyenne thought.

For a moment, Monica debated telling Cheyenne about her paying Cherry to kill CW, but she decided against it.

Now that she'd told Cheryl's story, she felt much better about what she was about to do. "Girl, I have to get outta here," Cheyenne said.

"That's right, you have to catch a flight," Monica said, looking at the clock on the Navigator's dashboard. "Girl, we been on the phone forty minutes; you better hurry up and get your ass up to that airport if you're gon' make the 7:30 flight."

Cheyenne checked her purse one last time making sure the scalpel's blade was pointed down, and away from the shiny gun lodged inside her purse. "Okay, girl. I'll call you when I land," Cheyenne said.

Chapter 39

*P*lans had changed. CW definitely had to die today, tonight. With someone like Cherry by her side, she might just pull this shit off without going to jail, Monica thought as she walked around to a side door of the church basement.

She was only a few feet from the door when her phone rang. "Shit!" She'd forgotten to place the phone on silent.

"Hello."

"What's shakin,' bacon?"

She looked at the Caller ID, not believing who was calling. "You black punk, bastard, bitch—"

"Ho-hold on, slow your roll, Sunshine," Jevon said.

"I thought you'd be somewhere sucking my husband's dick, or fuckin' him like you fucked me."

"Who the hell you think you—"

"You, I'm talkin' to yo' bitch-made ass. I can't believe you set me up. Knowing good and got damn well the mothafucka been trying to find a way to get rid of me since I tricked his ass into marrying me two and a half years ago."

"I know, I know. The man had some heavy shit on me. I had no choice."

"You had no choice! Nigga, you always have a choice. You just chose dick over pussy."

"No. I chose five thousand dollars and my freedom over pussy. Look, before you hang up. I need to see you," Jevon said.

"I don't see how you could've even fixed your face to say that shit. You need to see me." She giggled. "That's a joke."

"Look, Monica, I don't like that midget, Katt Williams-lookin' mothafucka, either, but it is what it is. I did what I did, and if you wanna know what I got on his ass, you need to come to the apartment, with no panties on."

"You think I'm gon' give you some pussy after the dog-ass shit you did to me?"

"Damn right, I do. And after I suck and fuck you until you cum a river, I'm gon' tell you what I got on that little mothafucka." He paused, smiling when she didn't respond. "And don't wear any panties under your skirt."

"How you know, I don't have on pants?"

"You never wear pants. At least whenever we hooked up, you never wore pants."

Fuck it, I'll get the gun later, she thought as she turned around. Besides, it isn't like any laundry would be done on a Sunday.

"So, you comin'?" Jevon asked.

"All depends," she said.

"On what?"

"If you have what it takes to make me cum."

"I can show you better than I can tell you. Use your key. And hurry the hell up, my dick is harder than quantum physics."

Chapter 40

"*N*o! No! No!" Bishop Wiley shouted. "Shit! Shit! Shit!" he said banging a fist on the desk he had set up in the temperature controlled AAA storage bin he rented, less than a block from the church megaplex. The small eight-by-ten storage bin was equipped with enough state of the art government-issue spy and surveillance equipment to make a James Bond movie. Desperate to add to the dirt he already had on Monica, he'd had camera's and listening devices installed all over the church, and the church administration building nearly a month ago.

"I can't believe this is happening to me?" he said, watching Monica walk back to her Navigator. He'd timed everything right, so what in God's name went wrong? Today was supposed to be his big day. He was supposed to become a living martyr. He was supposed to become bigger than Dr. Martin Luther King Jr., Malcolm X. They'd both been shot and they both died. He would live, thanks to the bulletproof vest and long johns he wore. He knew he was taking a chance, but he'd heard and saw all the tapes.

Cherry was going for a chest shot. He'd heard her explain to Monica that it was easier, safer, and deadlier, if you knew where and how to shoot.

The DVD he played in the car this morning was just ammunition to fuel her anger. He never meant to let anyone see the DVD after he got wind of Cherry's and Monica's assignation plot. Monica had no idea that the Bishop had bugged all of her purses. And the bishop had made sure he'd removed the bug that was in the purse she carried this morning. He didn't want the police to find it after they had arrested her for conspiracy to commit murder.

And that damn Cherry. The dumb heifer went the wrong way and ended up in the basement. *I should have drawn the idiot a map.*

After the last service, the bishop had driven to the storage bin as quickly and as unassuming as possible. The first thing he did was review the surveillance feed for the day. He saw Monica put the scope in the bathroom ceiling and he watched Cherry take the rifle and climb up into the vent. He didn't pick her up again until she left the basement laundry room empty handed. That's when he figured the gun was either in the air-conditioning duct, somewhere between the vestibule woman's bathroom and the laundry room, or hidden somewhere in the laundry room. He knew that either Cherry or Monica had to come back for it.

The cops he had on his payroll were less than a couple blocks away awaiting the bishop's call. Since he'd already had enough on Monica to get out of the marriage, he hoped Cherry would be the one to come back for the rifle, so he could send her right back to the nut house. And Jevon, well, he'd just have to figure out another way to get rid of him. Getting rid of Jevon was the only way for the bishop to be relieved of having to honor the agreement and paperwork they'd signed six years ago, giving Jevon a twenty percent interest in the Bishop C. Wendell Wiley Conyers Center City Mall. The mall build out had cost a little over three hundred and forty million. Jevon was as nutty as Cherry if he thought he'd see twenty percent of the profits for his measly two-hundred-fifty-thousand dollar investment.

Chapter 41

"**C**herry, I got one question for you. Why isn't my tongue tickling that pretty pink clit of yours?" Jevon asked Cherry while lying across the couch, one leg over the back stroking himself until Monica got there.

"Jordan, I got shit to do," Cherry said, speaking into her earpiece as she walked to the Delta Airline automated ticket machine.

"Ah, Sunshine, it can't be more important than doin' me."

Doc was so right. I can't believe I never saw it. And I can't believe I am actually going to give Jordan a pass. After Doc and that angry-at-the-world Monica explained the last seven years of the twins lives, I have no choice.

"Sunshine, guess what I'm doing now?" he asked.

"Jordan, I'm a grown-ass woman, okay? I don't play childish guessing games. Shit," she said, dropping her driver's license.

A man bent down and looked at the name on the license before picking it up.

Wild Cherry

"The only game I'm playing is golf, and I'm using Mr. Magic as the putter. Shit, girl, my dick's harder than quantum physics. Why don't you come over here and help me relieve some of this pressure."

"Dr. Jamison, here you are," the man said.

Jevon jumped up from the leather couch. "What he just call you? Where you at?" Did someone just call you Dr. Jamison?

Jevon didn't immediately know that Cherry had disconnected the call as soon as the man said Cheyenne's name. But as soon as he realized the line was dead, he pressed redial several times, and each time the phone went straight to voice mail. "Answer the got-damn phone. What kinda bullshit games you playin?" he said into Cherry's voicemail.

He didn't wanna give Cheyenne a copy of the disc so soon, but she'd pissed him off so bad he couldn't think straight. *Somehow her and Cherry hooked up, but that's okay, fuck both of 'em. I can't worry about that shit now. I gotta make up some shit on CW, some shit so bad that once Monica arrives, she'd suck and fuck me one more good time.*

Restless and not wanting to bust before Monica arrived, he got up, pulled his white linen shorts up and pressed play on the DVD player.

Moments later his favorite movie began to play. The Mack was a bad dude, boss pimp in his day, Jevon thought as he watched a young Max Julianne grace the screen. If the movie would've been made today, they'd have to recast Max Julianne's role. Yeah, he nodded, Jevon Hayes, the master Mack from way back.

I done had a threesome with two sisters. White sisters. But none of my exploits could compare with the shit I've

223

been pulling off for the past six months. Player of the year. Shit, I had to be player of the decade. I was fucking Bishop Wiley's wife—my wife's best friend. And I was fucking one of my brother's ex's, but she was also a patient of my wife's. And I had a threesome with both bitches. Now if that don't earn me a spot in the player hall of fame, nothing will. I bet Jordan will never top that shit. Damn, I almost forgot my wife. Hell, if it wasn't for me trickin' the bitch and pulling an Ike Turner on her ass six years ago, none of this shit would even be possible, he thought as he swung his leg back over the black leather couch.

Chapter 42

$\mathcal{T}$he nickel plated .38 felt warm and titillating in her hands. She didn't know much about guns. But she knew enough to put her hand over the top of it and pull the thingy back to load a bullet in the chamber.

Killing him would be easy now, she thought as she put the gun back into her purse. She kissed the picture of her daughter that she carried around in a plastic holder on her key chain. She looked up. "Lord, please keep Ariel and Jordan safe, and forgive me for what I am about to do," she prayed before putting the car in park.

For five months Jevon had had the apartment. And for five years she'd been his slave. Jevon had such an arrogant, I-don't-give-a-damn attitude that he'd even written the last rent check from their joint checking account to pay the rent on his not-so-secret apartment.

And his other women? Please. Cheyenne could care less about them. Heck, she didn't feel anything for Jevon, except raw, uninhibited hatred.

One thing she didn't do was blame him for screwing her best friend. No, that was all on Monica. Jevon was part rat, cat, dog, and snake. A scavenger. It was his nature to screw anyone and anything in a skirt. But Monica, after all they've been through, all they've shared, there was no way their relationship would ever be the same, despite what she had told her.

Finally, Cheyenne took a deep breath, massaged her temples, and got out of the car and started walking. Every time a foot landed on the pavement, a jolt of pain shot from her toes, to her head. She just wanted to sit down under one of the tall palm trees next to the gray and white stucco three-story building in front of her, down a Goody Powder, and relax for a few minutes before climbing the stainless steel stairs to Jevon's third-level apartment. But that was just wishful wanting, she thought as she braced herself on the stainless-steel railing while walking up the stairs. By the time she reached the apartment door, her head hurt so badly she was almost in tears.

She stood at the door, adjusting the blonde wig she wore. Should I knock? What if he asks who is it? What if he looks through the peephole and decides to act like he's not there? What if he tells me to leave? Maybe I should just shoot the damn lock?

She was running out of should I's and what if's when she heard and then saw the doorknob turning. After grabbing hold of the small, beige coach bag slung around her shoulders, she was slightly comforted when she felt the ridges of the gun's pearl handle.

As soon as the door started opening, she rammed her shoulder into it.

"What the hell..." He jumped back like he'd seen a ghost.

She slammed the door behind her.

"How did you..."

"The thirteen-hundred-dollar check you wrote from *our* joint account to the Palace Garden Apartment complex last month. That was real smart, genius."

"Fuck it." He shrugged. "You got me. I'm busted, now get the fuck out, before I..."

She took the gun out of her purse. "Before you what?" She pointed the gun at him. She had one eye closed as she aimed at his neck. "Before you what?" she repeated.

"Wh-what-what are you gon' do with that?" he stuttered while backing up. The twisted look and determined one-eyed stare on her face made him think that this time she was serious.

She matched him step for step. He took a step back. She took a step forward. "What do you think I'm gon' do with it?"

After running out of room, Jevon fell onto the black leather couch.

"Turn around!" she barked.

"Huh?" he asked.

She pulled the hammer back. "Turn... The... Fuck... Around. Now!

His mind was running a million miles a minute, but for the life of him he couldn't think of anything to say.

With lightning speed she reached down into the small Coach bag she had strapped over her shoulder and whipped out the six-inch, shiny, razor-sharp scalpel that Cherry had given her. Without warning or hesitation, just like Cherry taught her, she swept the blade across his arm.

"Got damn you." He fell to the ground face down, continuing to grab his arm as blood oozed from the deep wound the scalpel had made.

"This is the last time I will repeat myself. Now, turn over."

Without a word he rolled onto his stomach.

"Hands behind your back!"

"But my arm," he cried.

"Where's that baritone, manly voice? Huh, Jevon? Where's the voice you used when raping me, over the years."

"Rape? I can't rape my wife," he cried.

"Jevon. When a woman says... Why am I even entertaining your idiotic comments? You beat me mentally and physically, too many times to mention," she cried.

"What are you doing?" he asked.

She didn't reply. She just clasped the hand cuffs she'd brought around his wrists. Afterward, she stepped back and said, "Roll over and look at me."

He did as she commanded.

"No, you didn't just pee on yourself." She looked at the yellow stain in the middle of his white linen shorts. "Disgusting!"

"So, you gon' kill me? I-I mean right here with all these people living around me? All the noi-noise the gun'll make.

She smiled and brought the gun up from his crotch and aimed it at his head.

"Say something!" he pleaded with tears in his eyes.

"There is nothing left to be said. You've said it all. You've done to me what you've wanted to do for five years," She tapped the middle of his forehead with the gun's barrel. She leaned in, and whispered in his ear. "The only thing to do now is pull the trigger, love."

"Wait! Wait! Wait!"

She shook her head from side to side.

"Why? Why are you doing this?" he cried out.

Slowly she uncocked the hammer on the shiny .38. Then, she turned the gun around so the gun's pearl handle was pointed toward him. Ignoring his cries, she reached back and swung for his nose, but he turned and she gashed the back of his head.

"Ahhhhhhhhhhhhhhhh!" he shouted.

"Why did you trick me into believing that you were Jordan the evening I met you?" She hit him again. "Why did you rape me that night in the park when I still thought you were your brother?" This time his shoulder felt the butt of the gun.

"Ahhhh!" again he shouted.

"Why did you set Jordan up to take the fall for the bank you robbed? Why did you send that white girl in so you could make sure he was there when the police came to the apartment that night?" She raised the gun, poised to strike again. "Answer me!"

"You know why!" He balled up and squinted his tearing eyes, bracing himself for another vicious blow.

She let her arm fall to her side, while turning and looking toward the kitchen. He opened his eyes and turned his head toward her. He relaxed some, relieved that the onslaught of blows to his head, neck, and shoulders had stopped. And just as he began to open his mouth to try and reason with her, she turned back and wildly swung the gun at his head, busting him in the ear.

While rolling onto the floor screaming, he banged his knee on the couch. "Ahhhhhhhhhh, help me. Somebody, anybody, I don't know nobody, but somebody, please, this bitch is..." He stopped in midsentence as he turned his head.

Cheyenne had dropped to one knee, the scalpel's razor-sharp, diamond blade inches from his face. "Stop shouting, and answer my questions," she said with the calm of a sleepy philosopher.

"You already know the answers."

Ignoring his interruption, she continued. "If you say one word that doesn't have a ring of truth to it I'll come crashing down on your other ear twice as hard as I did the left one."

He started a little choppy, but after she feigned stabbing him in the eye with the scalpel, he spoke as if he were a college professor lecturing to an auditorium full of students.

The door bell chimed toward the end of his confession.

Jevon prayed that, somehow, someway, the police were at the door.

Her head turned to the door. Had someone called the cops? She turned back to him, aiming the gun at his face. "Say one word, and as God as my witness, it'll be your last," she said, thinking that if the cops busted in, she'd unload as many rounds into his head as she could before they shot her. She pulled the hammer back.

"Jevon, baby, it's me. Let me in. I left my key in the car."

Monica? Her key?

"Come on, baby. Open the door. Mommy is so wet out here."

After our talk. After she had realized that he'd set her up. And worse, all he's done to me. How could she? How could she look me in the eye? How could she?

"Jevon, baby, don't you wanna come take a dip in Momma nica's pool?"

She was still fucking him, Cheyenne thought as she kept her eyes and the gun aimed on Jevon, slowly back peddling toward the door.

Thinking that his only neighbor on the third floor of the relatively new apartment complex was at work, Monica continued. "All right, my fingers are about to be where Mr. Magic should be," she sang.

Cheyenne looked at her battered and beaten husband as he cowered on the floor next to the couch. "Mr. Magic," Cheyenne mouthed before placing the scalpel back inside her purse. With the gun behind her back she opened the apartment door, grabbed hold of Monica's dress at the neck line, yanked her into the apartment, and slammed the door.

Chapter 43

*A*ll first-class and medallion members can board now," a voice announced over the airport's intercom.

"Thank you, Dr. Jamison," the airline employee said as Cherry boarded the plane.

Minutes later, Cherry walked out of the restroom without the dark glasses, the wig, or the business pants and jacket she wore before entering the plane's, coat-closet-sized restroom. Now she wore her real hair, which was now cut into a cute, short afro, along with long red and white press-on nails, too-short jean shorts, and a matching Free Mumia Abu Jamal T-shirt. She looked like a 70's revolutionary stripper as she exited the plane. After a voice announced the last rows to board, she fell back in line, this time with her real I.D. and the same unobtrusive black carry-on bag with the clothes and wig she wore when she first boarded.

Wild Cherry

Monica tried to catch her balance but failed, falling onto the carpet. "Fuck!"

Cheyenne looked her up and down as Monica held her ankle while sitting on the floor. "You already did.

"What?" Monica said, rubbing her ankle.

Cheyenne looked over at Jevon. "And this, this animal." She again focused her attention on Monica. "Both of you fucked me, but the fucking is far from over."

High-yellow, light-bright, Pocohantus-lookin' bitch, was the first thing that came to Monica's mind after Cheyenne made her bust her butt on the living room floor. This was a different Cheyenne. Gone was the proper speaking, prim, doctor that Monica had come to know and love. Monica sat up and began rubbing the soreness out of her ankle. "What are you doing, Chey?" Monica asked as she found herself staring at the wrong end of a gun. Monica turned her head as if Jevon had some answers. She winced at all the blood on the side of his head.

Angry, and without thinking, Monica said, "You better pray to God you ain't made me sprain my got-damn ankle. Ho, don't you know I will kick yo' high-yella ass."

"I'm right here, Sweetheart." She placed a hand on her chest. "There's nothing between us but air and opportunity."

"Air, opportunity, and that," she pointed, "thing you have aimed at me," Monica said.

Cheyenne turned the gun over in her hand. "I don't need this to take care of you. What I need are some rubber gloves. That's what I wear when I take out the trash."

"Trash? Trash, bitch?" Monica slowly managed to get to her feet. "You married your man's brother and you call *me* trash?"

"Don't go there. You know why I married his ass," Cheyenne said.

"I've already gone there. Besides, just because he knew your little secret didn't mean you had to marry his ass. No, you just a college-educated dumb ho. The difference between me and you is that I'm a smart ho. Bitch, I married money." Monica looked over at Jevon, her eyes going from his head to his crotch. "Look at what you married, a broke-dick dog that'll fuck a tree if it had a hole in it." Turning back to Cheyenne with a quizzical look, she said, "and I'm trash? That nigga didn't have shit but a big-ass dick when you met him."

Jevon cut in. "You wasn't talking that shit when you was on your knees sucking the nut out of this big-ass dick."

Monica looked back at him. "Nigga, please. Shut your scary, half-a-man, down-low ass up before I tell your wife how hard you cum when I stick my dildo up your ass."

"I thought we were friends," Cheyenne said with a sad look on her face.

"We are, I mean, we were," Monica said. "And you shouldn't let a dick come between us."

"That's the way I expect low-life trash to think," Cheyenne said.

"Trash?"

"Is there an echo in here? Did I stutter?" Cheyenne asked.

Monica balled up her fist.

"Still, Monica, I'm married to," she waved the gun at him, "that dick."

"So the fuck what? It ain't like you love his ass. I'm married, too. But you think I give a damn who CW screws? Hell no."

"Loving him or being married to him is not the point," Cheyenne said.

"So, what..."

"The point is that you were my girl. We've been through hell together. We were both strung out on drugs. We helped each other pull through. No rehabs, just us."

"You were naked, stoned, and out of your mind, bent over a toilet stool with some fat pig ramming himself inside of you when I came and got you out of that frat house bathroom before the other twenty or so guys had their turn with you. Or, how about the time I took you to the emergency room when I found you in an empty apartment, half-dead from smoking some D-con-laced crack?" A look of disgust was plastered on Cheyenne's face.

"And now you're worse off than the crack-whore trash you were when I met you. At least back then you got ten dollars to open your legs and your mouth. Now you've stooped so low as to screw your ex-best friend's husband. For what, a few minutes of pleasure? An orgasm?"

"What's so wrong with that? You the one told me about his big-ass dick in the first place. You don't fuck him," she shrugged, "so I fucked him. All he is to me is a dick and a tongue. I married money, so I don't have to get it from elsewhere. All I need is a dick on the side and occasionally a wet tongue and I'm straight." She put a hand out in front of her. "So don't go judging me for having multiple orgasms with the nigga you givin' all your money to. A nigga can have the best dick and give the best head in the world, but that shit don't pay no damn bills. But dumb bitches like you do pay the bills and carry," she turned, "niggas like him. But I'm trash. You married and support trash, so what does that make you?"

"You..."

Before Cheyenne could get two words in Monica continued. "A trashcan, that's what you are. You can't even see that the nigga only with you because of your money and your standing in the community. Yeah, he making cake now, but he still ain't clockin' like you."

"I know all of this," Cheyenne said.

"Pssst. I can't tell." Monica rolled her eyes and put her hands on her hips. "You married, and are still married, to the punk, dildo-in-the-booty-ass nigga."

"I had to!" she shouted.

Monica took another step forward when Cheyenne lowered her head.

Cheyenne looked up and shook her head. "You don't understand; I had to," Cheyenne repeated.

"Bullshit! I'm so tired of hearin' that, *I had to, or he was going to tell on me, shit.*" She mimicked. "Bitch, you ain't gotta do nothing in this life but be black, and die."

"I already did." Cheyenne's voice, so loud and vibrant a minute ago, had now dropped to barely above a whisper. "I died the night he raped me in the park seven years ago. Now, I'm about to be reborn," she said in a trance-like state looking at the man she hated more than the devil himself. She smiled, bringing the gun up and pointing it for the last time at her husband.

Chapter 44

"Nooo!" Monica shouted as she barreled into Cheyenne's legs. Cheyenne lost her balance and sent the shiny .38 and her purse tumbling onto the carpet.

"What the?" Jevon said looking at the small tape recorder that slid out of Monica's Coach bag.

"What are you doing?" Cheyenne managed to say as she and Monica rolled around on the carpet.

"I'm, I'm... let go of my hair," Monica shouted. "You can't just kill him," Monica grabbed at the arm that had hold of her weave.

Suddenly, Cheyenne realized she had dropped the gun. "What have you done, girl?" she asked, looking up at Jevon.

"I'm saving you from yourself. He ain't worth it," Monica said.

"Bitch, shut yo' ign'ant ass the fuck up, both you bitches," Jevon said, now holding the gun in front of him.

Cheyenne and Monica froze, looking at Jevon wide-eyed.

237

"Ain't no fun when the dick got the gun, huh? Scary-ass bitch," Jevon said, looking at Cheyenne. "Oh, you wondering how I got the cuffs in front of me. Years of yoga, or did you forget?"

Cheyenne started to stand.

"Bitch, stay your ass on the floor," Jevon said.

Ignoring him, Cheyenne stood up, screamed, and rushed at Jevon's kneeling body.

With all his might, Jevon did a Barry Bonds swing and hit Cheyenne in the head with the gun and cuffs that were locked around his wrists.

*****

Bishop Wiley was loving every minute of what was going on inside the apartment. No one, not even Jevon, knew about the cameras and transmitters that were hidden in every room. When he hired Jevon to get close to and screw his wife, he had no idea that things would turn out this crazy. Then again, he did know how sick Cherry was. That's why he'd used his influence to have her conditionally released into his custody.

But Cherry was nowhere to be found. And that made him nervous. She was a cannon, one that had turned against him. From his perch inside the high-tech, air-conditioned storage facility, he continued to watch and listen to what was going on inside the small, one-bedroom apartment.

*****

"What are you doing, Jevon?" Monica asked.

"Just sit yo ass over there and shut the hell up," he said, waving the gun over at the couch he was sitting on a few minutes ago.

"Nah, negro, you on some dumb shit. I ain't signed on for this shit. I'm outta here."

"Bitch, you ain't goin' nowhere but over to that couch," he said, pointing the gun at her.

"Jevon, she needs help. Look at her." Monica said, sitting on the couch and pointing to Cheyenne's unconscious, half-naked body. "So you gon' rape her?" Monica asked as Jevon continued stripping the rest of her clothes off.

"Monica," he looked at her sideways, "look at me. Do you really think I have to take pussy?"

"Well, why are you... What are you going to do?"

"I'm about to teach the bitch a lesson. Why you trippin'? The funky bitch tried to kill me. She damn near cut my ear off and busted my head open." He shook his head. "Hell nah. You think I'm gon' let that shit ride?" he said, turning Cheyenne on her back and pulling down his shorts.

"Jevon, she's bleeding bad. Please let me call 9-1-1." Monica said, reaching inside her small purse.

"Put it down." He pulled the hammer back, and slung the handcuffs at her. "Now."

"Ow!" she shouted as the handcuffs hit her in the chest.

"Put 'em on, bitch."

"You don't have to do this."

"Don't make me knock your ass out. Keep running your mouth and you'll end up like her funky ass," he said, looking over at Cheyenne, who was laid out on the gray carpet, blood oozing from the gash in her head.

Monica began putting a cuff around her wrist.

Jevon took a couple steps forward. "Gimme your damn arm. No, better yet—"

"What are you doing?" Monica asked, completely in panic mode.

He twisted her arm behind her back and clamped one cuff on.

"Jevon!"

He placed a knee on her back and grabbed one of her legs, bent and pulled it toward her back, and placed the other cuff on her ankle. "Don't worry. I ain't gon' do shit to you." He took off his shoes and socks. "I just gotta make sure you don't try no dumb shit." He took off his socks and rolled them into a ball.

"You are cr—"

He stuffed his socks in Monica's mouth, before grabbing her chin and pulling it up so she could see his face. "And for the record, I can't rape my wife," he said while stroking his penis with his free hand. He took a few steps back over to Cheyenne's lifeless body. He opened his hands and spit in his palm. "Now it's time to wake the funky bitch up."

What have I done? Monica's eyes got wide as tears welled up in her eyes.

He grabbed Cheyenne's hips and kneeled down behind her.

Monica turned her head. She couldn't bear to watch.

Cheyenne stirred as he began to pull her up.

"Time to break in that asshole. Bitch, you ain't began to bleed yet," he said as Cheyenne's eyes fluttered open.

Chapter 45

*a*nger, disappointment, fear, rage, love, and an array
of other emotions twisted his heart and soul as he
listened outside of the metal garage door that Bishop Wiley
was behind.

Jordan had followed the Bishop from church to the
AAA storage facility. All he wanted to do was confront the
man. He just wanted the Bishop to tell him to his face why
he was exploiting his members and the black community.
He waited almost thirty minutes for the bishop before he
got out of his Dodge Ram and jogged behind a car entering
the security gates of the storage facility. It only took about
ten minutes to spot the bishop's black Bentley outside of a
large orange and white metal garage. Jordan couldn't even
imagine what type of surveillance system was behind the
metal door that he'd stood outside of for the last twenty
minutes. Nor could he imagine what would make a man go
to such links to spy on others.

Most of the conversation was choppy but Jordan had
heard enough to know that the woman he loved was in

trouble. Brother or not, no one was going to hurt Cheyenne any longer, he thought as he walked back to his truck.

Moments later Jordan was back at the metal garage with a prybar. "This is Jordan Hayes. Open up now or I'm calling 9-1-1," he said, deciding to try this tactic before forcing the huge metal door up.

"Give me a minute, son."

"I'm dialing 9-1-1," Jordan shouted.

"Okay, okay. I'll open up, but I haven't committed any crimes," the bishop said as the garage door went up.

"What in the hell are you doing? You sick bastard." Jordan said, looking at the small room that resembled a mini space station. "Why the hell have you not called the police?" Jordan shook his head. "Never mind. Where is this apartment?"

"I-I..."

"I-I hell," Jordan said before reaching out and grabbing the bishop by the back of his neck.

"What are you doing? I'm a man of God."

"Man of God, my ass," Jordan said, pushing him into a desk full of computer-like equipment.

The bishop crashed into one satellite-looking machine, starting a domino effect. "My equipment!" he shouted, as he watched sparks fly from the elaborate surveillance equipment that had fallen to the concrete floor.

Jordan reached down and grabbed the little man and pulled him to his feet.

"Where are you taking me?" the Bishop asked as Jordan led him by the neck.

A few minutes later, they were at his truck. "Get in, and move over," Jordan said as the bishop climbed in on the driver's side.

"You know this is kidnapping," the bishop said.

"You'll be able to add murder to the list if you don't direct me to the apartment where Cheyenne is. I know you play some part in all of this, and I promise you I will find out what, and when I do—"

The bishop interrupted. "Why not just call 9-1-1? We won't make it in time to save Cheyenne or Monica," the bishop said.

"You better pray we do, Bishop. You better pray like you've never prayed before. As God is my witness, if Cheyenne stops breathing so will you."

Chapter 46

*C*heyenne sat on her knees. She didn't say a word. Defeat was registered on her pale and bloody face. Cheyenne and Jevon's face were turned away from the front door. Monica was the only one that saw the apartment front door slowly begin to open.

"Bitch, it's time for you to learn how to treat your husband," Jevon said as he spread Cheyenne's butt cheeks.

Monica bobbed her head and attempted to scream but the socks in her mouth only let her release a low hum.

"Who's your daddy now, bitch?" he shouted, as he was about to ram himself into her behind.

"Move a muscle and it will be the last thing you ever do," a voice whispered in his ear.

Instantly, he let go of Cheyenne. Blood trickled down his chest. He was scared to breathe. Afraid that if he let out a breath too fast, the blade up against his neck would cut the skin more than it already had.

Cheyenne crawled from under him. Slowly, she continued crawling, dragging herself across the room.

"Now, I am going to move the blade from your neck, just enough so that you can speak," the voice said.

"Who the—Why—Wha-what are you doing?" he asked.

"Now what kind of idiotic question is that?"

Finally, he caught on to the voice. "Cherry, you got it twisted. I'm not who you think I am."

"You are exactly who I think you are. A low-life rapist taking up air and space in my world."

"I'm Jevon Hayes, not Jordan. I'm a twin. My brother is the one you want."

"Don't worry, I'm not gon' kill you. There is no way I'm gon' let a nobody like yourself send me back to that place. You're not worth it. I have too much work to do out on these streets," she said. Cherry reached inside her purse, "You're going away for a long time, asshole. The brothers I know on the inside will take good care of you. You may even be married off before your asshole is perforated or you contract HIV," she said, pulling her cell phone out.

"AHHHHHHHHHHHHHHHHHHHHHHHH!!!" a piercing scream caused Cherry to turn her head.

"No! Don't!" Cherry shouted as she dropped the scalpel and attempted to grab Cheyenne's leg.

Monica looked up and saw Jordan standing in the apartment doorway with tears running down his face.

Everything happened so fast that no one but Jordan could have stopped Cheyenne. Jevon just looked at his dick, which hung onto his body by a thin layer of skin.

In one stroke, Cheyenne had nearly castrated Jevon and slit his throat.

"Doc! Doc!" Cherry used her arm to beckon Cheyenne over to her.

Cheyenne shook her head, repeatedly, holding the bloody scalpel clutched to her chest.

Jevon made a gurgling sound as he held his arms out toward Jordan.

Jordan rushed in, right past his dying brother and took Cheyenne into his arms.

"I'm sorry, but, but I had to. I had—"

"I know, I know. I heard enough. I love you, Cheyenne. I am so sorry. I have loved you faithfully every second, minute, and hour of every day since the night we met, and I swear I will do whatever it takes to protect you," Jordan said, tears running down his face. "I'll never leave you again."

"Fuck all this love shit. Damn it, we don't have much time. Give me the fucking scalpel, Doc," Cherry said, reaching out to her.

"I thought you got on the plane," Cheyenne said.

"I did, but I got off. I didn't think you could go through with it. Besides, I didn't want you to. He ain't..." She looked over at Jevon. "Well, he wasn't worth it." She smiled. "But I guess I was wrong. You did it. But don't worry, you're still on that plane. Now give me your clothes. We have to hurry and you have to get the fuck outta here, Doc," Cherry said.

"Why? What are you doing, Cheryl?" Cheyenne asked.

Somehow, Cherry had got hold of the .38. Cherry turned and pointed the gun at Jordan. "Stop all the damn questions and give me your fucking clothes, Doc. You know I will shoot Jordan, so if you really love him you will save his life and unass that business suit, bra, panties— every damn thing."

Cheyenne began stripping.

"Cheryl, I swear to you, I am sorry. I have never forgotten what I let happen that day in the hotel. You could've been killed. I know what I'm saying are just words, and I know I-I never checked to see if you were all right, and my drug use is not an excuse. I just—"

"Got-damn, will everybody just shut the fuck up?" Cherry said as she stripped and threw her clothes to Cheyenne. "Don't ask, just put them on." She looked over at Monica while she dressed. "And you, sock mouth, open your mouth and I'll not only expose the plot on C. Wendell, but I'll come back for that ass, and trust and believe you don't want to be on my bad side."

Cherry pulled out the cell phone that was in her purse. "I slit the fucker's throat and I cut the nigga's dick off. That is what happened, and you all better not sway from that story."

Cheyenne was about to protest when Cherry interrupted. "This is not up for debate. Doc, you saved my life, literally. I was fucked up until you taught me how to forgive. Now that don't mean I won't ever take matters into my own hands again, but at least I have learned that people do change." She turned to Jordan nodded and smiled her approval before turning back toward Cheyenne. "And besides, your work is way too important for you to be in some jail or, worse, some loony bin. And don't worry about me." She smiled. "I'll be all right. I got some chips stacked and stashed," she looked in Monica's direction, "thanks to ole sock mouth over there."

"I can't let you do this, Cheryl."

She pointed the gun at Cheyenne. "Operator, my name is Cheryl Sharell, and I just slit a mothafucka's throat in Buckhead."

A few seconds passed before Cherry continued. "Jevon Hayes, and hell no I ain't gon' tell you where the body is. Tell your folks to leave the Dunkin Donuts and the Krispy Kreme, and do they damn job, shit." She disconnected the call.

"Just tell me why?" Cheyenne asked as Cherry made her way to the front door.

Cherry turned around. "Love, girl. That's why I've done all the dirt I have in my life. I love people so much, that, when I see evil, I feel like God has chosen me to destroy it at its core. The castrations are a message to all that watch the news and think about molesting or raping women and children. As you know, child molesters rarely do serious time, and rape often goes unreported. When it does get reported it is so embarrassing to the victim that further damage is done to their psyche, especially when they're forced to relive the episode at trial."

EPILOGUE

Two years later

" **H**oney, come quick," Cheyenne shouted into the kitchen where Jordan and Ariel were cooking.

"What?" he shouted, carrying Ariel into the theatre room.

"Look." Cheyenne pointed to the huge projector screen.

"Breaking news. We are coming to you live. You may have heard about the junior Senator from Mobile, Alabama, Jeffrey Charles. He was the man that was exonerated two days ago on an array of charges stemming from first degree murder to child molestation."

"Baby? Ariel, doesn't need to hear this. Tell me about it later. Come on, Princess, let's finish cooking," Jordan said, grabbing Ariel's hand and hurrying out of the large room with three rows of leather theatre chairs in it.

Later that evening, after Ariel was asleep, Cheyenne said, "Jordan, okay, you know about Senator Charles—"

"Yeah. He killed his wife and stored her in a freezer for four months after his wife caught him molesting their oldest daughter."

"*Allegedly* killed his wife," she interrupted.

"No, he did it. And even if he didn't, he'd been molesting his daughter for God knows how long. But in any case, that goes to show how the courts work. I still can't believe he got off on a technicality."

"He didn't get off. The maid found him dead in his home around six this evening."

"Good," Jordan said.

"Get this. He was castrated with a sharp object."

"Noooo... You think..." Jordan asked?

"I'd bet the farm it was our girl," Cheyenne said.

"She said she could take care of herself. I wish I knew how to get in touch with her, although I'm glad she hasn't got in touch with me." Jordan reached out and grabbed his wife's hand. "All we can do is pray for her, and pray for Monica's soul, too."

They spent a moment of silence gazing at the stars while lying out on the patio couch.

"Baby, I don't care what they say; I still don't believe Monica committed suicide," Cheyenne said.

"Me either, but what can we do but pay our respects at the funeral tomorrow?" Jordan said.

"I bet anything that Bishop Wiley had something to do with Monica's death. They hated each other. The only reason they stayed married was because of his money and status in the community. But she was planning to take him down and expose him for the fraud that he is, before that day at the apartment."

"Too bad you and her never spoke again after Jevon—"

"Yeah, too bad," she said, cutting him off before he spoke of his twin's death. "But I did send her an invite to our wedding. It wasn't my fault that she didn't show."

Jordan had never told anyone, not even Cheyenne, about the Bishop's little high-tech surveillance station at the AAA storage facility. He didn't know why he'd kept it to himself, but he just did. After his brother's death, he just wanted to forget everything and concentrate on the future. Finally he was happy. He was married to his soulmate, and the adoption of Ariel would be final in a couple of days. Everything was good in Jordan Hayes's life. He was even enrolled at Georgia State University. He was majoring in religion and minoring in African-American studies. He wanted to teach an Afro centric version of theology in a church he planned to start. One patterned after Solomon King's New Dimension's First Church of God.

*****

The next day, in the church compound parking lot from inside a red ten-year-old Toyota Camry with deep tinted windows, Cherry watched a cavalcade of Bentley limo's pull up to the front of the church. Moments later, Cherry watched the ever-so popular Bishop TJ Money get out of the last limo, followed by Bishop C. Wendell Wiley.

"Eeny, meeny miney mo," Cherry pointed back and forth at the two bishops, "Catch a ho by the toe, if he hollers cut him some more," she continued, trying to decide which one was next on her hit list. "Eeny, meeny miney mo."

Book Club Discussion Questions

1. Why do you think women like the ones in Crazy Craig's stable, stay with and give their money to a man who is as sadistic as Craig?

2. Do you think there are women in the streets that have pimps like Crazy Craig? And what would you say to these misguided Queens, if you were given five minutes with them?

3. Did Jevon love his brother Jordan? And if you said yes, how could he do to his brother what he did if he truly loved him?

4. What would you have done if, you were Cheyenne, and you were put in a situation where you had accidentally caused a child's death, because you were high on illegal prescription drugs; you covered your involvement with the child's death up. And years later you told a man that you thought you loved, but he used that information to blackmail you into marrying him, having his child, and using you and your hard earned money for his own gain.

5. If you were in Cheyenne's situation, confused, but in love, would you have gone to Jordan and told him everything while he was in prison.

6. In Wild Cherry a homeless man proposed the question, if you died today, how do you think you would be remembered? What is your answer? How do you think you would be remembered, and how do you want to be remembered?

7. Why are there so many gifted Black men on drugs? And why do you think so many have to go to prison and

become reformed? And the ones that are reformed, how do you think they change inside a place infested with the criminal element, or shall I say what the courts deem as the criminal element.

8. What do you think about Cherry's brand of justice?

9. Do you think Cherry was insane?

10. Are there really people of the cloth out there as corrupt as the Bishop C. Wendell Wiley? And if so, why can't their congregations see them for who they are?

11. What would you have done, if a teenage girl came up, propositioned you for money for sex, and even offered a threesome with her own mother?

12. What is Wild Cherry really about? How many hidden messages are there, and what are they? And how could this book help women?

13. Why do you think that Cherry did what she did for Cheyenne at the end of the story?

14. Would you like to see more of Cherry in the future? If so would you like to hear the story of her father the "Son of Cool?" or would you like to see what happens next in Cherry's life?

Turn the page a read the prologue for the sequel to Jihad's 2008 blockbuster hit **PREACHERMAN BLUES.**

PREACHERMAN BLUES II

A Change is Gonna Come

Coming to a store near you and on <u>www.jihadwrites.com</u>

09/09/09

PREACHERMAN BLUES II
A Change is Gonna Come

"When a person places the proper value on freedom, there is nothing under the sun that he will not do to acquire that freedom. Whenever you hear a man saying he wants freedom, but in the next breath he is going to tell you what he won't do to get it, or what he doesn't believe in doing in order to get it, he doesn't believe in freedom. A man who believes in freedom will do anything under the sun to acquire... or preserve his freedom."

Malcolm X

Prologue

"*Y*ou're right, GW. But who knew that it would come so soon. Our plan was for President Bakari to die after serving half of his first term, not nine months after taking office."

The former 41st president of the United States stood at the window with his hand on his chin. His eyes were looking out at the helicopters and the private jets that were shadowed by the hundred acre forest that hid the Montana Tri-lateral commission compound, but his mind was being absorbed by the domino of problems caused by him and the tri-lateral commission failing to interfere with the last presidential election. Hell, Bakari fit the profile. Mixed heritage, raised by his white mother, and white grandparents, Harvard grad, member of all the right organizations, nothing prepared him or the men in the room for what was going on now. Hell, no one gave Bakari an ice cube's chance in hell of beating Clinton in the primaries. The NAACP didn't even support the man.

"Dammit GW," Bradley Rockefeller slammed his fist on the round table he and the others sat around. "Your son.

Wild Cherry

It's all his fault. We," he made a sweeping arc with his arm, "all of us in this room put him in office, not once, but twice we put that idiot son of yours in office.

GW, still didn't turn around. He acted as if he hadn't heard the former senator and billionaire.

"This is not the time to place blame. I told you all when I was in office that my son was going to be loyal to *us* and only *us*, but," GW turned to face the other eight most powerful men in the world, "I also said that he wasn't ready."

"But—"

"Please, let me finish." GW placed both arms on the oak round table. With calm he continued. "From day one, that we decided no to interfere with the last election, we knew that if we let a black man become President, that we'd have problems."

"Mansa Hussein Bakari, are you kidding me? What in the God friggin' hell?" Conrad Meyer, the world's biggest media and entertainment mogul ranted. "All these friggin' billions of dollars we spent on Islamic propaganda and instilling the fear of God in the American people, and the got damn idiots vote for a nigger named Mansa Hussein friggin' Bakari."

"Calm down Conrad. Please." GW pleaded. "In the last eight years all of us have boasted record profits from the war, and we stand to earn at least another seven to eight hundred billion each over the next four to five years. We've been together for over forty years, Vietnam, Desert Storm, nothing we've ever engineered brought us the kind of money and power that we are about to have in a few years. After the mess of the 2004 presidential election, we couldn't take a chance on interfering again. We all agreed that Bakari or Clinton being elected would buy us time with the world's foreign leaders."

"He's right." Prince Nathan, the Queen of England's last living son said. "Way before the election, we decided that

2

we needed a good PR person in office. Someone that would get North Korea, Iran, Russia, and Nigeria to drop their guards long enough for us to take them out like we did Iraq." Prince Nathan stood up. "We knew that we had to do something strategic and different to get the world to view us in a different light, a positive light. Hence, the election of a Black into office. Not since JFK have we allowed the people of your country to elect a president."

"Now you see why?" Rockefeller interrupted.

"It was a means to an end of Middle Eastern oil dominance," GW said. "We've all made sacrifices for this day and the day we all are working so hard to see. Am I proud of Vietnam? Am I proud of Desert Storm? Am I proud of nine eleven? Am I proud of this Iraq war? No. But these are disasters that we had to engineer to get us closer to world dominance. Millions have died. Americans, and others, and many more will die before we," he made a sweeping arc with his arms, "can bring the world under one ruling faction, *us*.

"Enough with the state of the union address GW. Bottom line is," Conrad paused, "the friggin' nigger president is out of control. None of our intelligence prepared us for former governor and religious leader Solomon King."

"I beg to differ with you," Rupert interrupted. "I have two words for you, Jeremiah Wright. I made sure that man was plastered all over my network and I made sure CNN and the others followed my lead. Now, if Bakari was mentored by that man, then as history has shown us," he placed a finger in the air, "it's only a matter of time before another Jeremiah Wright-like influence surfaces in Bakari's life. And he has. We should have handled Solomon King long ago, before we took out Cochran, Brown, or Lewis. We could have even set it up like we did MLK. It's bad enough, Solomon King's One Free movement is still growing, but now he has Bakari considering reparations for slavery that ended almost 150 years ago."

GW interrupted, "Hell, the conversation of reparations have come up many times over the last thirty years, but this is the first time the new bill being drafted has a serious chance of passing. Imagine all the blacks that will take advantage of free education, and health care. Imagine all the future Bakari's." GW, shook his head. "No, we have to act now, we have to immobilize the president now. Bakari must not live to see the end of the week. And we have to help a new black leader rise."

"Another Black," Rockefeller interrupted.

"If we don't want a potential civil war on our hands, we have to groom another Black to take Bakari's place."

"GW, seriously, you know the Blacks don't stick together. They'll burn up their communities and cry for justice, at best, but they won't do anything beyond that."

"It's not the blacks we need to worry about. It's the blacks, whites, and Hispanics. They all put Bakari in office, and that Michael Moorer and Bill Mahrer will rally the whites behind a potential civil war between government and the common people."

"Even though it will look as if Bakari died of natural causes?" Gerald Greenspan asked.

"There are enough conspiracists with the people's ear, such as Moorer, and Mahrer, that could cause a civil meltdown. But if we get behind, say another Black leader, a religious leader and make him the voice of black and white America we can do extensive damage control and have a man we can control in office in three years." GW smiled, "And I have just that man.

STREET LIFE

by JIHAD

*S*treet Life is a journey into the struggle of a young black male raised in America's inner city streets. Not since Donald Goines and

Claude Brown has there been a comparable story written from the male perspective about the inner city streets. As the merry go round of life in the hood is relived; explanations will become evident for the events and circumstances that lead so many to the prison-gates. In this true to life story a vivid, colorful picture is painted of why growing up in an environment where happiness is sought in the bottom of liquor bottles, needles and dope sacks is just ordinary life in the hood. Whenever one tries to break the cycle, unseen hands pull at him to continue the course he was conditioned to complete. It takes a conviction and lengthy prison stay for Jihad to change his thinking and change the course of his life.

ENVISIONS PUBLISHING, LLC
P.O. Box 83008, Conyers, GA 30013

Enclosed: $_____ in check or money order form as payment in full for book(s) ordered. FREE shipping and handling. Allow 3-5 days for delivery.

ISBN 978-1601620071 STREET LIFE $12.00

Name_____

Address_____

City_____State____Zip_____

RIDING RYTHYM

By JIHAD

*R*iding Rhythm is a love story set in the early 1970's and 80's. Rhythm is a college student in D.C. who learns of Moses King, the man who started the Disciples, a street gang in Chicago. After reading his court case she writes him. The letters start to flow back and forth and Rhythm becomes an attorney to fight the system that has incarcerated the man she falls in love with. Moses' estranged brother,

 Bishop Solomon King, seems to have his own agenda as he becomes a controversial and popular Baptist minister. Lawrence One Free is Moses' friend and mentor in Atlanta Federal Pen whose guidance causes Moses to change the direction of the Disciples. Pablo "Picasso" Nkrumah was of the 12 kings in the Disciples. When Moses goes down he organizes the Gangsta Gods, a rival gang. The Chicago police and the F.B.I. stay one step ahead of Moses, Picasso, Law, and Solomon, until Rhythm brings them together and teaches what the power of love and unity can accomplish. When Rhythm touches the lives of these men, everything changes and all hell breaks loose. Rhythm's heavenly flow shows hell what love can do.

ENVISIONS PUBLISHING, LLC
P.O. Box 83008, Conyers, GA 30013

Enclosed: $_____ in check or money order form as payment in full for book(s) ordered. FREE shipping and handling. Allow 3-5 days for delivery.

ISBN 978-1893196483 RIDING RYTHYM $12.00
Name_____
Address_____
City_____ State____ Zip_____

BABYGIRL
By JIHAD

$\mathcal{T}$his is a story of a girl born to L.A.'s rich and elite. She's known simply as Baby Girl. Circumstances force her and mother to end up living on the streets among Atlanta's homeless. Soon they befriend Shabazz, a white-heroin addicted scam artist who thinks he is black,

and his best friend Ben, a scholarly alcoholic who analyzes everything. Baby Girl's mother is killed. She is now being raised by Shabazz and Ben, learning the intakes of hustling. She has it all until another tragic event causes her to take on a new fight. She is a female Robin Hood, robbin' the rich and givin' back to Atlanta's homeless and dejected. So, eventually she recruits and trains women like her, beautiful in appearance but poisonous to the touch.. Baby Girl will make every woman wonder, is it really a man's world or is it a woman's world where men only exist if women let them?

ENVISIONS PUBLISHING, LLC
P.O. Box 83008, Conyers, GA 30013

Enclosed: $\$$_____ in check or money order form as payment in full for book(s) ordered. FREE shipping and handling. Allow 3-5 days for delivery.

ISBN 978-1893196230 BABY GIRL $12.00
Name_____
Address_____
City_____State____Zip_____

M V P

By JIHAD

*M*VP is the story of two best friends and business partners. Jonathon Parker and Coltrane Jones have a history. The best friends and business partners have been involved in everything from murder to blackmail, whatever it took to rise they did. Now they're

sitting on top of the world, heading up the two most infamous strip clubs in the nation, the duo has the world at their feet. But now they both want out for different reasons. Coltrane is tired of the drug game, He's hoping to settle down with the new woman in his life. Jonathan, now a top sought after criminal attorney, is ready to get out of the game, that's because his eye is set on the Governor's Mansion. With the backing of major political players, he just might get it. There's only one catch. Jonathan has to make a major coup... bring down his best friend, the notorious MVP, Coltrane

Jones. As two longtime friends go to war, parallel lives will collide, shocking family secrets will be unveiled and the game won't truly be over until one of them is dead.

ENVISIONS PUBLISHING, LLC
P.O. Box 83008, Conyers, GA 30013

Enclosed: $_____ in check or money order form as payment in full for book(s) ordered. FREE shipping and handling. Allow 3-5 days for delivery.

ISBN 978-0-9706102-1-8 MVP $12.00
Name_____
Address_____
City_____State_____Zip_____

PREACHERMAN BLUES
By JIHAD

Best friends...Mega preachers...One good....One evil....
As kids, Terrell "TJ" Money and Percival "PC" Turner had one goal – become big-time preachers. But once they accomplished that goal, heading up One World Faith; the largest church in the

Southeast, the best friends disagree on just how they should be leading their flock. TJ is living up to his name and looking to capitalize on a congregation more than willing to shell out big bucks for a "man of God". Percival tries hard to walk the straight and narrow, but eventually the lure of the bling leads him astray.

Can either survive?
When PC tries to right his wrong ways, the battle lines will be drawn and best friends will see sides of each other they never knew existed. Soon, TJ gets down and dirty – pulling up every trick and devastating secret to keep his holy money train rolling. Will Percival learn the hard way that TJ is a sinner who doesn't want to be saved? And if he does, will it be in time enough to stop tragedy from turning his own life upside down? When the dust settles someone will definitely be singing the Preacherman Blues.

ENVISIONS PUBLISHING, LLC
P.O. Box 83008, Conyers, GA 30013

Enclosed: $_____ in check or money order form as payment in full for book(s) ordered. FREE shipping and handling. Allow 3-5 days for delivery.

ISBN 978-0-9706102-2-5 Preacherman Blues $12.00
Name_____
Address_____
City_____ State_____ Zip_____

WILD CHERRY

By JIHAD

Cherry is one bad chick. That's no surprise since she's the granddaughter of one of the most thorough hitmen in history, Daddy Cool. An NFL Superstar and bad boy himself, Jordan Hayes is about to find that out the hard way when he decides to

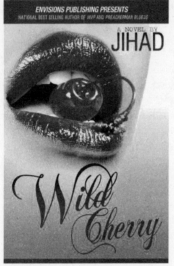

make Cherry a pawn in his game of lust, drugs and lies. After Jordan moves on, he forgets all about the girl he once called "Wild Cherry." But Cherry hasn't forgotten about him. In fact, he's all she can think about as she does her time in a state mental institution.

You play...you pay

Jordan's twin brother Jevon has been living in his twin brother's shadow for years. When an encounter with a beautiful young lady opens the door for him to not just follow in Jordan's footsteps, but assume his whole identity, Jevon jumps at the chance. But Jevon is in for a rude awakening when he discovers the real reason his new woman is called "Wild Cherry."

ENVISIONS PUBLISHING, LLC
P.O. Box 83008, Conyers, GA 30013

Enclosed: $_____ in check or money order form as payment in full for book(s) ordered. FREE shipping and handling. Allow 3-5 days for delivery.

ISBN 978-0-9706102-3-2 Wild Cherry $12.00

Name_____

Address_____

City_____ State_____ Zip_____